THE Lady URSULA

ANNE R BAILEY

INKBL❦T PRESS

Please note this book is written in UK English (example: color is correctly spelled colour).

To all my readers. Thank you, truly.

Bluehaven Series

The Widowed Bride

Choosing Him

Other

The Stars Above

You can also follow the author at: www.inkblotpressco.ca

England

STAFFORD
CASTLE

KENILWORTH
CASTLE

LONDON

THORNBURY
CASTLE

WARBLINGTON

PENSHURST
PLACE

Ursula Pole Family Tree

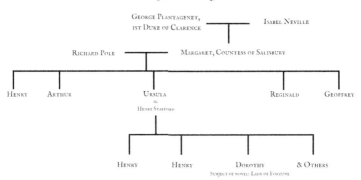

GEORGE PLANTAGENET, 1ST DUKE OF CLARENCE — ISABEL NEVILLE

RICHARD POLE — MARGARET, COUNTESS OF SALISBURY

HENRY — ARTHUR — URSULA
m.
HENRY STAFFORD
— REGINALD — GEOFFREY

HENRY — HENRY — DOROTHY
SUBJECT OF NOVEL: LADY OF FORTUNE
— & OTHERS

Henry Stafford Family Tree

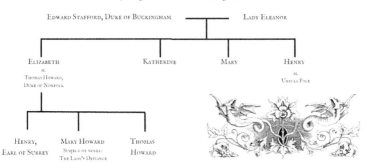

EDWARD STAFFORD, DUKE OF BUCKINGHAM — LADY ELEANOR

ELIZABETH
m.
THOMAS HOWARD,
DUKE OF NORFOLK
— KATHERINE — MARY — HENRY
m.
URSULA POLE

HENRY,
EARL OF SURREY
— MARY HOWARD
SUBJECT OF NOVEL:
THE LADY'S DEFIANCE
— THOMAS
HOWARD

AUTHOR'S FOREWORD

In this novel I have strived to stick as closely as possible to the historical records available.

However, some dates, especially birthdays, may be inaccurate, as they were rarely recorded or were given as estimates. I have found that sources can contradict each other.

Ursula's oldest brother, Henry, was born in 1492, Reginald in 1500 and her youngest brother in 1504. Sources claim Ursula was already alive at the time of Reginald's birth, so I have picked 1499 as the year of her birth.

As with most novels set in this period, you will find several characters named Henry, Jane, Mary, Anne, and Elizabeth. Naming conventions of the time dictated that children were often named after members of the Royal Family. Where possible I have done my best to distinguish these characters by changing their names slightly. For example, Harry rather than Henry.

The following is not an extensive list of my sources, but I would like to share them for those who wish to do further reading and research for themselves:

Hall, Edward. Hall's Chronicle: Containing the History of England, during the Reign of Henry the Fourth, and the Succeeding Monarchs, to the End of the Reign of Henry the Eighth, in Which Are Particularly Described the Manners and Customs of Those Periods. Google Books, J. Johnson, 1548

Harris, Barbara. "The Trial of the Third Duke of Buckingham-A Revisionist View." The American Journal of Legal History, vol. 20, no. 1, 1976, pp. 15–26. JSTOR, https://doi.org/10.2307/844847. Accessed 25 Oct. 2023.

Pierce, Hazel. Margaret Pole, Countess of Salisbury, 1473-1541: Loyalty, Lineage and Leadership. University of Wales Press, 2009.

"The Field of Cloth of Gold." Historic Royal Palaces, www.hrp.org.uk/hampton-court-palace/history-and-stories/the-field-of-cloth-of-gold/

Weir, Alison. Henry VIII. Ballantine Books, 18 Dec. 2007.

Weir, Alison. Mary Boleyn : The Mistress of Kings. Random House Inc, 2011.

The Lady Ursula concludes my Royal Court series. I started in 2017, and six books later I feel I have unearthed the stories of some of the lesser-known women of the Tudor court.

From the bottom of my heart, thank you for all your support.

I hope you will go on to check out my other novels, including my upcoming novel *The Saxon Queen*, set in 1100, during England's early medieval period. It follows the beginnings of Matilda of Scotland (or Edith, as she was known before her coronation) and her marriage to Henry II.

CHAPTER 1

Today, her future would be secured. Last night, she'd dreamed she was swathed in red velvet trimmed with ermine, a coronet on her head. She could still feel its delicious weight.

Yesterday, as Lady Ursula Pole, she had none of those things. Her existence was of minor note. But later today, as Lady Ursula Stafford, wife of the Duke of Buckingham's heir, she would leap over the other ladies of the realm. At the age of nineteen, she would take precedence over her own mother. The thought was ridiculous and pleasing, all at once.

The maids moved about her with pins and ribbons, making adjustments to her gown. Another was waiting impatiently with a comb and rose oil to brush through Ursula's sandy-brown hair. Ursula was certain there had never been a more beautiful bride on her wedding day. Certainly not one more eager.

Holding out her hands in front of her, Ursula flexed her slender fingers, admiring her rings. She was still getting used to their cumbersome weight, but for the life of her she wouldn't remove them. She would be a duchess one day, and she wanted the whole world to know it.

Her mother strode into the bedchamber, and all activity stopped as the servants made their bows and curtseys. Hampered by the seamstress, Ursula nodded her head respectfully. As she studied her daughter, Lady Margaret Pole, Countess of Salisbury, cut a severe figure in her dark gown edged with gold embroidery. At last she gave an approving nod. To the others she commanded, "Carry on, we will have to be at the chapel in no time at all."

Ursula straightened, her heart pounding as she willed time to move faster. Closing her eyes in a silent prayer she tried to regain her composure.

The gown she had chosen to wear today, with her mother's approval, was made of crimson velvet stitched with pearls and lined with cloth of gold. Never in her life had she worn such a gown. And it was new, not someone's cast off. Soon Ursula would get used to such luxuries. After the King's wife, sisters and daughters, she would be the foremost woman in the land.

Just the thought of it made her want to squeal. Instead, she dug her fingers into her palm and smiled serenely.

She heard men's voices outside her chamber doors, and recognised one as Edward Stafford, Duke of Buckingham — her future father-in-law.

Her mother, with her keen hearing, frowned and strode to the door. She opened it with a flash of her wrist, as if it was nothing. "My lords, may we help you?" she asked imperiously.

Lord Edward peered around her. "We came to see if the bride was ready. All this delay is making me hungry."

Ursula could only imagine her mother's disapproving frown. Margaret Pole preferred to ensure that everything was done just as it should be. Ceremony was important to her, as was her wealth and status. God knows, for a long time she'd been without both. Now she clung to her traditions and wealth as if they would buoy her against the storms that had destroyed her family.

"The bride is nearly ready, Your Grace," Margaret informed the Duke primly. "Is the groom impatient?"

Lord Edward let out a puff of air. Since arriving with his retinue and son in tow, it had been clear to all that he wished to conclude this business as soon as possible. The Duke wished to be at court with the King, not tucked away in the countryside attending weddings. Had it not been for Ursula's large dowry, perhaps he wouldn't be here at all.

Her brothers, Lord Montagu and Sir Arthur, had tried to keep him busy hunting in the deer park and hawking, but to no avail.

Ursula sniffed, annoyed that he wanted to hurry this along. This was a momentous occasion. All decorum must be observed to give the event some gravity, and here the Duke was, falling short of her expectations.

Oh, how she wished the wedding could have taken place at court. The King and Queen might have attended, and they would have dined at Westminster and danced beneath the beautiful vaulted ceiling.

But on this matter the Duke of Buckingham had been insistent.

Her mother shut the door and turned to Ursula, her

expression one of barely contained irritation. "You will have to learn to stand your ground."

"Even though I must cleave to my husband?"

Her mother's lip twitched. "Of course. It is your duty as his wife to obey him, but there's nothing wrong with nudging him down the correct path, for his own benefit as much as your own and your family's."

"I understand, Lady Mother."

Margaret motioned to a maid to bring over a sealed chest. She opened the lid to reveal a chain of rubies and pearls interlaced with sapphires.

As her mother clasped the necklace around her neck, Ursula felt the cool touch of gold on her skin.

"You look like a duchess already," her mother said, placing a hand on her cheek. "May God bless you."

Ursula, now fully dressed, curtseyed gracefully.

"I am proud of the lady you've become, and I know you will go forth to a glorious future. Never forget you are a Pole, and from my line descended from Plantagenet princes." Ursula saw the gleam of pride in her mother's eyes.

The door to her chamber opened once again, and her brother, Lord Montagu, appeared to escort her to the church. This was it. The time had come. Without hesitation, nor a single tear shed for her childhood, Ursula wrapped her arm around her brother's and allowed him to lead her towards her future.

At the doors of the church the priest waited, along with the Duke's household. Ursula caught a glimpse of her husband-to-be, Henry Stafford, wearing a suit of cloth of gold, edged with crimson. They were a perfect pair, and she preened at the thought of how well they would look standing side by side.

Casting a glance at the waiting guests, Ursula saw her brother's new wife, Jane Neville, standing at the front. They had been married just two weeks ago, but their wedding had been conducted quickly, without any fuss. Jane's wedding clothes had not been this sumptuous. There was an edge of contempt in her sister-in-law's smile as she met Ursula's gaze. Was she jealous?

There was no time to dwell on it. Keeping her head proudly high and her eyes fixed ahead, Ursula found herself handed over to her betrothed. He was taller than her but not by much. His even features and bright blue eyes made him look all the more handsome, and Ursula was satisfied. After all, her husband could've been anyone, even some old earl; and it would've been her duty to marry whoever her mother chose.

As she studied him, he peered back at her. His smile was genuine, and she guessed he was pleased by her too.

They turned to the priest and the ceremony began. A small gold ring was placed on the Bible, and the congregation was asked if there was any reason why this marriage could not go ahead.

They said their vows on the church steps and then were ushered inside. Kneeling together before the altar, the priest blessed them and conducted Mass.

At last they rose, husband and wife. The only thing left to do was to consummate the marriage to make it legally binding.

But first there was the banquet.

Ursula and Henry were given the honour of sitting at

the centre of the raised table. They ate off gold plates and drank from fine Venetian glasses. These luxuries would be packed up to accompany her to her new home.

Her mother had spared no expense to show off the wealth and power of her family. The windows of the great hall were draped with new curtains of russet damask silk, and the walls had been freshly plastered and painted with elaborate scenes of lions stalking their prey. Above them, servants had hung garlands of flowers from the rafters. As the guests sat listening to the speeches about the union of two great families, servants began arriving with the food. There was a never-ending stream of dishes, each more delicious than the last, including pies, and roast meats of every kind. But Ursula was so excited she could only pick at the food.

Then the musicians up in the gallery strummed a tune and the dancing began.

Henry stood. "Shall we dance, my lady?"

Ursula giggled and nodded. The wine had not been watered down and she felt lightheaded as he led her to the dance floor. Only a year older than her, Henry was a good dancer, though not as graceful as her brother Arthur. Every time the dance brought them together she felt a thrill. This was her husband, the handsome knight, and she was the beautiful damsel. She envisioned him jousting at a tournament, her favour tucked in his doublet for good luck. He would emerge victorious, and when his eyes found her in the crowd he would bow to his lady love and say that without her, he would never have won.

Such daydreams put a wide smile on her face as she spun around, trying to recall the steps in the dance.

His hands were always there to steady her, and she felt she loved him all the more.

"I am glad it's you I wed," he murmured.

"I am glad too," she said, blushing.

"Mary Talbot has nothing on you. She's sallow, and I never saw her smile."

At his words, she sobered. What did he mean? "Mary Talbot?" she parroted.

Henry shrugged. "Yes. My father wished to marry me to the Earl of Shrewsbury's daughter, but they couldn't agree on the dowry."

Ursula's mouth was dry. "Ah."

"I suppose your mother will pay any price to strengthen her position. The king may have restored her to favour and granted her lands but nothing is certain. Even so, I know your lineage is nothing to balk at. It's nearly as impressive as mine." He flashed her a smile, as though what he'd said was a compliment and not an insult.

Struggling to keep her composure, Ursula was glad when the dance ended and she could return to her seat. She did her best to keep her temper. It would ruin everything if anyone saw her displeasure. But then again, wasn't everything ruined anyway?

She bit the inside of her cheek and reached for some candied almonds.

Marriages were always made to further the family's fortunes. Jane Neville was an heiress; once her father passed away his castles would go to Jane and her heirs. They would make Ursula's brother, Lord Montagu, rich, and eventually add to the family holdings. Ursula was bringing a tidy fortune to the Buckingham estate, to bolster their reserves. This had never been a love match, but she had never imagined she was the second choice.

It stung, and dampened her enthusiasm. And her husband — she side-eyed him — had he told her that to be cruel? Or was he genuinely unaware as to how she might react? Maybe. He simply did not care about her feelings.

Ursula's gaze travelled to her mother, seated next to the Duke. They both seemed satisfied, leaning towards each other as they talked.

She strained to hear snippets of their conversation over the din of the hall.

"This is as it should be," the Duke said, waving a hand towards the gathering. "The true nobility honoured and the rest kept in their place. We have no use for upstarts whose lowly beginnings should make them beneath our notice."

Her mother inclined her head. "With this union we are strengthening the bonds and uniting two powerful bloodlines."

"And who knows what the future will bring."

From her vantage point, Ursula saw her mother tense. The Duke liked to tread on dangerous ground. The lack of a male heir for the King and Queen was a constant discussion across the kingdom. Yet, the Duke often went too far. He also forgot how loyal Lady Margaret was to Queen Katherine of Aragon, having served her since she arrived in England eighteen years ago.

"Only God can know," her mother said, unwilling to continue the conversation. She artfully changed the topic to his new building project at Thornbury.

Ursula shivered as she let her own imagination take flight. If Henry Tudor failed to produce a son, would the crown go to the Duke of Buckingham? He was certainly a powerful nobleman, and his Plantagenet blood would make him a contender for the throne. By extension, Ursula and her husband could inherit the crown. It was a treasonous thought, but it set her heart racing with excitement.

That night as she retired for the evening, she thought of the great destiny before her. They had prepared the bedchamber with flowers, wine, and a tapestry of a knight singing ballads to his lady. It all felt ridiculous now. The noblewomen teased her and laughed at her flushed cheeks. It was useless to blame the wine. Ursula wasn't nervous; she'd bribed a maid for information, far more than her mother had given her but she felt no eagerness. All she could think about was that she was the second choice. However, her desire to one day be a duchess had not cooled.

As Henry led her by the hand towards the bed, she turned her thoughts to the jewels she would buy and the gowns she would wear. This brought her more pleasure than any of Henry's ministrations. With the business done she felt a burst of happiness they had sealed this marriage. Of their own accord, her hands reached for her husband's shoulders, feeling the powerful muscles beneath. She had nothing to compare this to, but she thought it was tolerable and her husband well-formed. As she slumbered, her dreams found a new perch as she envisioned Henry as the future King of England and then, surely, he would conquer France. With her at his side, they would create an empire.

After the wedding, Henry and Ursula travelled to the Duke's grandest estate, Penshurst Place. Heavy rains had made many of the roads impassable as they travelled north-east, away from the coast. For a new bride this was hardly the honeymoon she had expected. Her husband had been distant, and despite visiting her bed some nights, he didn't bother riding beside her while they travelled. Ursula was left in the care of her mother-in-law, a cool, detached woman with no interest in making small talk. Lady Eleanor was perfectly content riding silently every day.

"Father is taking me to court," Henry said one morning as he was leaving her room.

"When?" she asked, too shocked to form a coherent sentence.

"Today. We will come to the crossroads and our party will divide. You and my mother will go on to Penshurst."

"I should like—" she bit her cheek, refusing to beg to be allowed to accompany her new husband.

"You'll have plenty to do getting settled in. My sister Katherine is there too. I'm sure the two of you will find something to do," he said, sounding uninterested. "I'll come bid you farewell when it's time. Good day, wife."

She nodded, accepted his kiss and watched him go. It was wrong to hate her husband, but in this moment she feared she did.

For the first time in her life, Ursula had someone of similar age and rank living with her. She and Katherine took to each other immediately. Despite being older, Katherine, with her mild manners, was happy to defer to Ursula.

It was unusual that at twenty-two, Katherine was still unmarried. Even Ursula's match had been unusually delayed, as most noble ladies married before the age of nineteen. One day, as they rode out with an escort to go hawking in the early morning light, Ursula asked why that was.

"Father says, after the dowry he paid for Elizabeth he's in no rush to see me married," Katherine said, stroking the dark grey feathers of her bird. The falcon pulled at his jesses, impatient to fly.

"I am certain he will find you a good match."

Katherine's lower lip trembled.

"What's wrong? Surely you don't want to spend the rest of your days in your father's house."

"No. But I —" she gave a small shake of her head. "I cannot speak about it."

Ursula wanted to press her further, but they'd reached the edge of the deer park.

They stopped in the shadow of the trees. An accomplished horsewoman, Ursula held her merlin, Gem, aloft on a thick leather glove, the reins of her horse in her other hand.

"There's plenty of quail this time of year," the huntsman said, coming up to her, all the while studying the area. "Shall we set the hounds loose?"

Ursula inclined her head, letting loose her merlin. The huntsman gave a whistle and the dogs took off at a run, disappearing into the field. It wasn't long before prey scattered to avoid their snarls.

Ursula watched Gem zero in on her prey. With a dip she manoeuvred herself to intercept a fleeing sparrow. Her talons found their mark and Ursula, beaming with triumph, summoned her back.

The falconer came forward to take the sparrow from the merlin.

Gem returned to Ursula's glove, and she spoke to the bird softly, marvelling at the blue gleam of her feathers. Bigger than males of the species, Gem was at her peak. She'd been one of a pair of merlin given to Ursula and Henry as a wedding gift. Katherine had borrowed the male, Silver, but was having trouble managing him.

"Let him loose. He can find himself a nice fat partridge or a rabbit, if he fancies."

Removing his hood, Katherine let him fly. Lighter and faster than Gem, Silver kept his eyes peeled for prey. He dived into the grass and from the sounds that emanated, it seemed he had caught something. Again the falconer ran to retrieve the kill.

"Well done," Ursula said to Katherine, when the falconer showed her the young quail it had brought down.

Satisfied with their catch, and with most of the prey now scared off, they hooded the birds and returned home.

As they rode side by side at a leisurely pace, Katherine finally turned to Ursula, ready to share her feelings. "The Earl of Westmorland was my father's ward for many years."

Ursula inclined her head, aware of this already.

"Before my older sister was married, the Earl had thought of marrying her. But my father found a better match for Elizabeth."

Unease filled Ursula as she saw Katherine's pinched expression and the white-knuckle grip on her rein. "And now?"

"Father hasn't said anything to me yet, but I have heard that he wishes to finalise a marriage between the two of us."

Ursula couldn't see what the problem was. There had

been no pre-contract from the sounds of it. "Is there something about him you object to?"

A sob escaped Katherine's lips, and she quickly put a hand over her mouth to stifle the sound. Tears were threatening to escape the corners of her eyes. "There's nothing to object to, except for the fact he's in love with my sister."

Ursula gasped. "But she's married now. Surely this was merely a passing fancy? In time he will come to love you too."

Having calmed herself, Katherine shot her a look. "You don't understand what it's like to be the youngest sister. I always have my sister's cast offs. But I want to be loved for myself. If I marry him then he will always be comparing me to her."

Ursula fixed her gaze straight ahead. This could very well be true, but Katherine was jumping to conclusions.

"We can speculate all day if you wish, but you cannot be sure this would be the case. Try to consider the positives. Marrying him will make you a countess with all the wealth and prestige that entails."

"My sister will one day be a duchess."

"Yes, she might outrank you, but that doesn't mean she will be happier than you. She's far from home, whereas you will be close by, even after your marriage."

To drive the point home to her sensitive sister-in-law, she leaned over in her saddle and gave her hand a squeeze. It startled Ursula that she had said such a thing. Yet, she couldn't deny how all the little trinkets and gowns she bought as Henry's wife only gave her a fleeting moment of pleasure. As quickly as the realisation struck her, she pushed it away.

Life at Penshurst held a gentle, consistent rhythm. There was always something to do, whether it was hunting or hawking, picnics or walks in the garden and, of course, the endless needlework.

Yet, Ursula found she no longer had the energy to ride out with Katherine, and she'd developed an aversion for the decadent food served at dinner.

Her mother-in-law summoned her to her presence chamber one day and examined her closely.

"Have I done something wrong?" Ursula said, thinking about the gold necklace of sapphires she'd ordered from a jeweller, and her new petticoat of green brocade.

"When was the last time you bled?"

Ursula blinked at the crude question. "I-I don't remember."

Her mother-in-law tutted in annoyance. "Your chambermaid says you haven't had your courses for eight weeks now. And you are sick in the mornings and low on energy. Is this correct?"

Ursula was taken aback. She hadn't been aware there were spies among her maids who would report everything to her mother-in-law. But she bit her tongue and answered, "Yes, Lady Eleanor."

"Then it is likely you are with child. Congratulations. I shall write to my husband and son to tell them the good news." She patted Ursula's cheek as though she was a well-behaved horse.

Ursula left her mother-in-law's chamber in a daze. She had barely had time to get used to being a wife.

Katherine was confused as to why Ursula was so distraught over the news, and tried to comfort her. But it was hard for Ursula to admit to her complex feelings. She was scared and angry, but also thrilled, and filled with pride that she had accomplished her duty so swiftly. On her wedding day, she had envisioned days spent getting to know her husband; that he would dote on her and love her. She'd dreamed they would be summoned to court, and all would envy their beauty and wealth.

That had not come to pass, and it was a bitter pill to swallow.

Worse news was yet to come, as the Duke announced Katherine's marriage contract was finalised. Soon, Ursula would lose her only companion too.

Despite Ursula's concerns, the days flew by. After a time she regained her energy and put all her effort into helping Katherine prepare for her nuptials.

As luck would have it, Ursula could not attend the wedding. It didn't matter how much she begged, she'd entered her period of confinement and was unable to leave her darkened apartments. Her mother-in-law visited her from time to time to check she had everything she could want; she did not sit with her to gossip but merely inquired if all was well and if she needed anything. Ursula had to rely on letters, and hearing news second-hand from her lady's maid.

"She looked beautiful, my lady," her maid said. "A beautiful blue velvet gown trimmed with marten fur."

"And the groom?"

"Handsome." The maid smiled.

Ursula was tempted to ask if they looked happy, but that was beside the point and an improper question to ask her servant. Besides, how could she have known?

"Bring me my writing desk," Ursula said, intent on writing Katherine a lengthy letter. With it she would send more gifts for the new bride.

It made her sad to consider that once she left this darkened room, she'd be alone in the house with only her mother-in-law for company.

They placed her son into her hands and she marvelled at the new life she'd created. He'd been cleaned and wrapped in soft linen. Soon he'd be swaddled up tight but for now he was free to kick and mewl as he pleased. There was a fuzz of gold on his head, and she wondered if he would take after his father rather than her. A fierce love overwhelmed her and when the midwife came forward to take him back she wanted to claw at the woman.

Some of this must have shown on her face because the midwife smiled and said, "Lady Eleanor wishes to take him to see his father and the Duke."

With a nod Ursula let him go. Her eyes never left him as he was handed over to Lady Eleanor, who'd been waiting nearby in the birthing chamber. Her mother-in-law spared her a moment's thought and smiled. "You've done well," she said, feeling the weight of the babe in her hand.

Then she went to show the baby to Ursula's husband and father-in-law. Later, Ursula would learn that the pair had spent the morning playing cards and drinking so much wine that when her mother-in-law appeared with the baby, they fell over themselves trying to stand.

In the darkened chamber, Ursula was urged to rest as the servants moved about replacing the soiled linens and cleaning everything. Her mind was hazy from the spiced ale they urged her to drink, and she was exhausted after being awake all night. Everything had been like a dream — a long and painful one.

It was a man's duty to defend his kingdom and go to war armed with a sword, spear, or longbow. Women faced childbirth in much the same way. It was a matter of endurance and determination — yet for all that, luck played such a huge part in it. Ursula felt she'd like to try her luck with a sword next time.

Her lady's maid, Maggie, sponged her face with cool water.

"Is there anything you need?" she asked.

"Sleep," Ursula muttered.

Looking over her shoulder, Maggie said something to the midwife who must have agreed, because she said, "Sleep then, my lady."

As Ursula closed her eyes she thought she could hear the distant sounds of celebration. It was all for her son. A faint smile danced across her lips as she drifted off to sleep.

"I am glad to find you looking so well, madam," Henry said, as he entered her rooms for the first time since her confinement began.

Other husbands broke with tradition, but he had not seen her until she had been churched. He'd sent a letter by the priest who came to say Mass for her every day, and a present of an emerald pendant. After their wedding they'd gone their separate ways; even her pregnancy had not changed their relationship. Life resumed as if nothing much had happened. She and Henry came together when it was necessary on formal occasions, but he preferred to roister with his friends. It wasn't in his nature to be attentive. Often he'd ride off for weeks to go hunting at his father's various parks. Privately, Ursula disapproved of his behaviour, and it was a blessing to be left to her own devices. He was of an age to be learning the business of running his father's estates, but he didn't have the inclination, and Ursula was beginning to fear he lacked the capacity for it. Like a child, he expected everything to be done for him so he could be free to enjoy himself.

All in all they were considered a successful match. She knew she should be grateful he treated her with kindness and respect. But it still rankled her that he had a freedom she would never possess.

Her husband moved about the room as the maids folded away the heavy curtains that blocked the light from the windows. Used to the bustle of the tiltyard and activity of a hunting party, he was ill at ease in the stillness of the women's quarters.

"I've stitched new collars on your shirts," she said. "They are on that table over there."

"Ah, thank you," Henry said. His eyes flicked to them, uninterested.

In her dark confinement chamber she'd stitched away at them for hours on end. Was this to be her thanks? She did her best not to frown. It did not matter. She'd done it more to fill the time than to please him.

"They tell me your father is sending you to Thornbury," she said, hoping to get more conversation out of him.

"In a few days." He looked at her with passive interest. "You will have the baby to look after," he added, as if to assuage his own guilt.

"Of course."

He came forward and kissed her cheeks. "I shall write to you and you must do the same. Tell me how our son fairs."

"I'll be happy to do so. He shall grow up to be strong, like his father," Ursula said, with motherly pride and ambition.

The compliment sat well with Henry, who puffed up. "Yes, exactly. It just goes to show how God favours us. They say the Queen has lost another child, though she never told the court she was with child in the first place."

"Poor lady." Ursula put a hand over her heart. Now that she had a child of her own she understood the plight of the Queen.

Her husband, on the other hand, scowled. "She is an old crone, and you know what they say about the Tudor line?" He leaned forward to whisper, lest they be overheard.

"What?" Ursula asked, despite the danger of hearing such treasonous words.

"They are cursed. My father told me so. There won't be a male heir."

Ursula gasped, and put her fingers to his lips to stop him from speaking further. "If anyone heard ... Besides, the point is moot. The King had a son born to him by Bessie Blount last year."

He merely grinned. "A bastard, and who knows if he

will live. Everyone says the King cannot have a son. Look at *our* bloodline. We are strong and virile. None of us have trouble begetting male heirs. It's a sign from God." Henry gazed at her fondly, and bridged the space between them by placing his hand lightly on her stomacher. "I shall visit you tomorrow night. Perhaps we shall make a brother for little Harry to play with."

Inwardly, Ursula grimaced. The thought of repeating the ordeal of pregnancy so soon did not appeal to her, but she didn't pull away. He kissed her lips and then left the room without a backward glance. She tried to forget the conservation, for as much as she might secretly desire to become Queen, it was a different thing to voice this aloud.

Her mother, having gone through a period of exile and destitution without royal favour, was much more circumspect than Henry about voicing her opinions of the Tudors. By contrast, the Staffords were vocal in their disdain for the King's policies, and sometimes even the King himself. Their power and wealth gave them that privilege, but for how long would the King turn a blind eye?

Hating to be upset, she cast his words from her mind. It was innocent blustering from her husband. Foolish, but innocent.

Today she would undertake to set her rooms back in order, but first she wished to check on her son in his nursery.

He was allotted his own room, with a small staff to look after his every need. Everything had been arranged by Lady Eleanor, from the guard at his door, to the rockers and nursemaids. But Ursula had insisted on selecting the wet nurse herself. Agnes, a woman from the village with a spotless reputation, had soft, gentle features. She was recently widowed, and not much older than Ursula herself.

Now, as she entered the rooms, she saw Agnes sitting by the fire with little Harry in her arms.

"He was hungry, my lady," Agnes said, looking up.

Ursula nodded and sat on a stool beside her to watch as her son latched on to Agnes's breast. A twinge of envy hit her at the sight, and she tried to push it away.

"His lordship eats well," Agnes said, stroking his head. Her own daughter was sleeping in a crib nearby. She was a tiny creature but looked healthy. Ursula had promised the girl a small dowry, and to take her into the household as a chambermaid when she grew up.

Ursula smiled. "That is good to know. He needs to grow up fast. I just promised his father he will be a great warrior."

The wet nurse laughed. "He will for sure. He kicks about so fiercely when they free him from his swaddling bands." Agnes yawned and shifted Harry to her other breast.

When he was done, he was half asleep and ready to be returned to his cradle. Ursula waved away the nursemaids who came forward and took him in her arms. He was a month old now and felt heavier in her arms. Milk dribbled from the corners of his mouth and she smiled at him, using the sleeve of her gown to wipe it away.

She placed him gently in his crib, gently stroking his cheek with a finger. His eyes closed and soon he was dozing. He was an angel. With nothing left for her to do, Ursula stood and entreated the servants to continue their vigilance for his well-being.

As she was leaving, Lady Eleanor entered the room,

followed by the ladies in her train. Ursula knelt and greeted her mother-in-law. "Your Grace, I bid you good day."

Eleanor's eyes flicked over her and nodded her approval. "You look well." Already she was looking past her to the enamelled crib.

"My son has just finished feeding and is sleeping. We should let him rest," Ursula said, staking her claim on him as his mother.

Lady Eleanor was unimpressed by her blustering. "Perhaps you'd like to take a turn in the knot gardens? The roses have bloomed early this year. It will reinvigorate you."

Ursula was gently being put in her place and dismissed.

"I shall. Thank you for your concern, Lady Eleanor." She was forced to step aside so her mother-in-law could go past.

She went to her room to fetch a shawl, and to ask Maggie to accompany her.

The sky was blue overhead, and there was birdsong all around as little sparrows darted about. She stopped to pet a tomcat lazing on a warm stone in her path. Its dappled white coat was soft and it purred contentedly at her ministrations. Eventually, it rolled over so she might scratch its belly.

"You are king of your domain," she said, smiling down at him.

"Don't be fooled, he's a vicious hunter."

Ursula looked up and saw the master gardener approaching. He bowed to her respectfully.

"Is he indeed?"

"The best we've got. Keeps the mice and other vermin

away from our seed stores and the kitchens as well. As you can see, he's quite plump."

Ursula smiled and scratched behind his ears. "Yes. Well, he deserves to reap what he sows. I must congratulate you on the spectacular garden. I've never seen such beautiful roses." She stroked one nearby. The unusual petals were a dusty apricot colour with a rosy pink centre.

"Thank you, my lady. His lordship is sending me to build an intricate rose garden at Thornbury. It'll be even more breathtaking than the ones here at Penshurst."

"It will be a paradise," she said, wistfully.

The gardener excused himself.

A wave of melancholy washed over her. Everyone was going. She had done her duty and everyone was pleased with her; there was no reason to feel sad. Yet, she felt cast adrift, as if everyone would prefer it if she was tucked away in some storage room until she was needed again.

Ursula clasped her hands tightly together, willing the darkness that descended over her to dissipate.

"I wish to return to my rooms," she said to her maid. "Summon the seamstress. I think a new gown is in order and it shall match this beautiful garden." With that she spun on her heels and marched determinedly to her rooms.

Penshurst Place was a marvel. The ancient sandstone fortified palace had been expanded and improved over the years, but the medieval foundations remained. The hall sported a beautiful vaulted ceiling with an intricately carved chestnut roof. Arcade windows let in plenty of light, illuminating the hall beautifully. The walls were painted with frescos and hung with rich tapestries, and the family banners hung on the far wall, where family members dined on a raised dais so that their tenants and visitors could see them.

From the hall she went up the stone steps to the solar and private apartments beyond. In the gallery, Sir Thomas Boleyn, a man of many talents, was helping the Duke manage the estate, stopped to let her pass. Her eyes drifted to the large sheaths of rolled up parchment in his hands.

"Good day, Sir Thomas. I suspect those are plans for the renovation projects at Penshurst?"

He bowed his head. "They are indeed." He waited, and Ursula took some pleasure in knowing she outranked her father-in-law's manager and that he had to wait upon her pleasure.

He was a man of many skills and, if she recalled correctly, married to the Duke of Norfolk's sister. And the Duke of Norfolk himself was married to Henry's older sister, Elizabeth. Wherever she looked there were relatives, or people with close family ties. The Boleyns were a family on the rise, powerful in their own right. And yet, here was Thomas waiting for her to dismiss him. A muscle in his hand twitched with impatience at her prolonged silence.

Her smile widened a fraction; the taste of power was sweet indeed. "I would like to discuss the changes to be made to my son's rooms. I fear they will be inadequate as he grows and, God willing, has more siblings."

"Certainly, you shall have to discuss—"

She interrupted him. "— with you, when you have a moment. The Duke ought not to be troubled over this, and I have the authority to oversee my son's upbringing. As well as the funds."

"As you wish."

"Until tomorrow then," she said, and he nodded curtly.

Ursula continued on her way, pleased with herself. She might have overstepped the mark and maybe even attracted his ire, but she didn't care. One day she'd be Duchess, and if her husband was to be believed, maybe even more. It behoved the likes of Thomas Boleyn to accommodate her.

In her rooms she was gratified to see that everything was returned to its original place. Her tapestry of the Battle of Troy with the silver embroidery was back hanging on the wall. Her room had been aired out and there was a fresh scent of clean linen and herbs in the air.

She glanced at her writing desk and noted the pile of letters waiting for her. And the seamstress was waiting in the wings to be summoned.

One thing at a time. With a smile, Ursula turned to the seamstress, motioning her to approach with a flick of her wrist.

"I had the most wonderful idea for a new gown. The colour of apricots, with an outer layer of tulle, embroidered with roses, doves and pomegranates in honour of the Queen. I believe there was some such fabric in the store-room somewhere. If we cannot find any that will suit, then we shall have to buy it."

"Will this be a court dress?"

The question was innocent, but it put a damper on her enthusiasm. Indeed, her father-in-law continued to have no desire to bring her to court. Henry had been little help on the matter as well.

"You should be here," he'd said, patting her cheek. "The court is full of danger."

Ursula's lips had pursed in displeasure, but he'd kissed

her and promised she could go for Christmas. That promise hadn't been honoured, because of her recent pregnancy.

"Yes," she said to the seamstress. "Make it grand enough for court. Even if I never go, I might as well be dressed in the finery that befits a future duchess."

"As you wish, my lady." The seamstress bobbed a curtsey. "I shall bring you sketches, the latest from France. We can model the gown to whichever style you prefer."

The idea of being dressed so fashionably put a smile on Ursula's lips, and she nodded.

Next she turned to her letters. There were several she hadn't bothered reading since the birth of her son. Recognising the seal of her mother, the Countess of Salisbury, she tore into it and read the glowing praise lavished upon her.

My brave daughter,

I hear you have been delivered of a healthy son. I congratulate you both but especially you. With this act you have proven to the world how worthy you are to be the future Duchess of Buckingham...

The letter went on instructing her to take care of herself and the baby. There was a promise of a gift to follow, but it had yet to arrive.

Ursula knew this marriage had been a triumph for her mother. Yet she was still coming to terms with her new role. At least life at Penshurst was pleasant and she had every luxury to distract her. Certainly her parents-in-law held her in higher esteem now that she'd done her duty and given Henry an heir.

A servant entered the room and said, "My lady, Sir Robert Gilbert wishes to speak with you."

Ursula put aside her mother's letter. "I can see him now. Show him in."

Sir Robert was her father-in-law's chancellor, in charge of the Duke's finances and administering his lands and other legal matters. He entered, dressed in black, his features hidden by a full beard, his hair streaked with silver.

"Thank you for seeing me at such short notice." He bowed his head.

Despite his deference, she sensed his displeasure with her. In his hands he carried a large book, and now his fingers tapped it. "Some matters have come to my attention that I wish to speak to you about."

Ursula took a seat and waited for him to go on. Perhaps it was rude of her not to ask him to sit too, but Sir Robert seemed perfectly content with the higher vantage.

"My lady, your marriage contract provided you with an allowance of seven hundred pounds per annum. Your mother has added land that generates an additional profit of five hundred pounds, to be divided between yourself and your husband."

"That is correct," Ursula said primly. She wished he wouldn't drone on; would just get to the point.

"Well, I have calculated your expenses. In the last two quarters you've spent a significant portion of that allowance."

"Have we?" She was surprised. Then again, she hadn't exactly been frugal when it came to ordering new gowns, filling the stables with new horses that took her fancy, and refurnishing her rooms here at Penshurst. Then there was her son's nursery.

"You alone, my lady, have spent six hundred pounds. I

am not even including your husband's extensive expenses in this. Nor his gambling debts."

Ursula could hear the judgment in his tone, but what he failed to understand was that she had to keep up appearances. This was her due as the future Duchess of Buckingham. She couldn't be seen counting pennies like a peasant girl.

"I am afraid you will have to make reductions."

"Everything I have spent has been to benefit this family," she said, though doubt began to creep in. It was true she had to maintain an air of grandeur about herself, but how many of her purchases had been made out of pure boredom? She cleared her throat. "Of course, I will take greater care in the future, but there have been a lot of expenses to manage. Perhaps the Duke would like to increase our allowance. After all, now with his grandson here, matters are different. Soon he will need tutors, horses of his own, servants and staff — would you speak to him?"

He looked exasperated. "My lady, spending money at this rate is not only ill advised but dangerous."

She pursed her lips as she listened to him droning on about how finances of a great household like this worked, as if she didn't know. As if she had never seen an account book in her life.

"Sir Richard, thank you for bringing this to my attention but I believe I have offered you a solution. If you cannot find the time to speak to the Duke, I have no qualms about doing so myself."

He blanched, his lips pinched into a thin line of disapproval.

"I assume you've already spoken to my husband about

this as well. I don't see how he can't live on the remaining three hundred and fifty pounds. He doesn't maintain a large retinue of his own and he has rooms here at Penshurst. Perhaps you can persuade him to reduce his trips to London and stop gambling. I have my son and myself to look after."

"But the clothes and the—"

"I do believe I am finished, Sir Richard. Thank you." She dismissed him.

Anger flashed across his features but he didn't dare contradict her. Bowing, he left in a huff.

The Duke always made a big show of his wealth. If he expected his only son and his wife to live in poverty, he was making a mistake. Privately, she didn't know why she was pushing for this. As she constantly reflected, her purchases brought her temporary happiness. However, asserting herself and demanding to be acknowledged — now that kept a smile on her face for days.

She turned to her lady's maid. "We'd better use the blue velvet for the cushions rather than the embroidered silk." It was significantly cheaper but still striking.

"Very good, my lady."

With that taken care of she turned back to her other unread letters. Jane, her brother's wife, had written to her a note of congratulations. At the end of the letter she also told Ursula she was expecting a child in the autumn and hoped it would be a fine son like Ursula's Henry.

Ursula sniffed. There would be no finer child than hers. Then she smiled at herself for her fierce loyalty to him. Was this how her mother felt?

She pulled out fresh sheets of paper to write her replies, and signed her name with a formal flourish. She poured hot wax onto the letters and pressed her insignia ring into it. The solid gold ring had been a wedding gift, the embossed chevron pattern of the Stafford coat of arms overlaid with her initials: *U S.*

Once the wax was dry, she summoned one of her pages to despatch the letters. Satisfied, she retreated to her adjoining bedchamber to rest before supper. Ursula found she couldn't sleep. Instead, she envisioned the carved chests and other furniture she would commission for her son, then thought of gowns for herself, fine silks and soft damask. Hats and scarfs lined with soft sable furs for winter, and dainty, soft slippers for her feet. She sighed at the luxury of it all.

Everything was within reach. Yet some unnamed desire chased after her, nipping at her heels.

She turned on her side, shutting her eyes tight.

All would be well.

CHAPTER 3

1520

The Duke returned to Penshurst Place with a large retinue of men, but Ursula's husband had remained behind at court. It was mid-May, and the whole court was preparing to embark on a voyage to France. Ursula wondered if she would be included in this, but dared not let herself hope.

"Henry sends you his love," the Duke said, as he peered at his grandson sleeping in his cradle.

"I hope he is well," she said. Her words were courteous, but she couldn't bring herself to ask more.

"Yes. Yes. I hope the King will take him into his service in some capacity soon. But what shall we make of this little man?" the Duke said, a tenderness she'd never seen before in his voice. He bent low and carefully picked up the sleeping infant.

Little Harry scrunched up his face, upset about being disturbed, which only made the Duke's smile deepen. "He knows what he wants."

The unusual tenderness moved Ursula to tears. His

father should be cooing over him like this, but Henry had only seen him twice. She hid her face and wiped away the tears before her father-in-law could see.

"You've heard about the meeting between our king and the King of France, I assume?"

"This was Wolsey's doing, was it not?"

"You are well informed." He set the babe down. "It was his policy that brought this about, but we will use it to our advantage. To that end, you shall be in the Queen's train when we set out to Calais."

Ursula's eyes widened. "I-it would be an honour."

"We will remind everyone that there are still noble families in England. As such, you must be aware that all eyes will be on us. I don't believe you will give me a reason to be embarrassed."

"No, my lord," Ursula said, bowing her head, the picture of obedience.

"Good. This trip home was twofold. When I leave at the end of the week you shall come with me, as will Lady Eleanor."

"And little Harry? Shall he come too?"

The Duke took a moment to consider but shook his head. "No. He's far too young. There's no point exposing him to the dangers of travel."

Ursula looked down at his peaceful face and knew she would have to steel herself to be separated from him.

"If there's anything you need, just order it," the Duke said at last, and left the room. He paused in the doorway and said, "You are a good wife and mother. I am pleased with you."

For him to deign to say this to her was the ultimate

compliment and she felt her chest swell with pride. That niggling voice at the back of her mind quieted to a mere whisper.

Ursula threw herself into preparations with frantic energy. There was so much to do and so little time. Gowns were brought out of storage, each finer than the last, and the treasury was opened to retrieve jewels too precious to keep lying about.

She would spend her time in Calais decked in gowns of cloth of gold and silver. Lady Eleanor was in her element, preparing her chests with the precision of a military commander. Ursula envied her expertise and speed.

"You shall learn with time," Lady Eleanor said one evening, as they sewed fine black lace onto their husbands' collars. The King wore such shirts himself and Queen Katherine was renowned for her fine needlework. Looking at her own neat stitches, Ursula knew she had nothing to be ashamed of, but neither was the design spectacular. The Duke had requested it, as such a show of finery would bolster his own prestige and importance.

"There seems to be a never-ending inventory you store in your mind," Ursula said.

She shrugged, nipping at the thread. "I've been doing this for years, and I never know when my husband will require some little thing or other." She passed the needle to one of her ladies to re-thread.

Her eyesight, which had apparently never been good, had grown worse in the last few months. If there was an ounce of embarrassment in her, Ursula couldn't see it. She retained her dignity and never let this impede her.

Watching her mother-in-law, she took the lesson to heart and hoped to embody the same stoicism.

"Do you think we will be at court more after this little sojourn to France?"

"I expect not," Lady Eleanor said. "The Duke feels it is best we stay in the country. There's much to do and oversee. Those we employ will always find ways to cheat us. That being the case, could there be a better solution than to turn to one's family to manage things?"

The question was rhetorical, so Ursula remained mute. She felt this was unfair, as the men were free to do as they pleased and attend court without worry. Even her mother often trusted others with the management of their estates. But arguing with Lady Eleanor would accomplish nothing, and would attract her ire. It was better to put such matters aside.

After a time, Lady Eleanor broke the silence. "You've heard of Lady Anne Fitz Allen, the Duke's sister, have you not?"

"Vaguely. I heard she was banished from court for some misdemeanour." Ursula hated admitting she didn't know what that was, but was more interested in finding out than in tending to her pride.

"But she never went home," Lady Eleanor said, her gaze flicking to her as though Ursula was supposed to understand something from this.

"Was she ill?"

"No. She was confined to a nunnery, and not long after, she perished." Lady Eleanor grimaced. "Her story is one of many examples you should keep at the forefront of your mind when you long for public life. The court is a dangerous place and there are many temptations and traps for you to fall into. Anne had been my friend before her marriage. We were of one mind. What led to her tragic end, I will never know. This was years ago, in the early days of King Henry's reign. She was a new bride, brought to court to serve in the Queen's household. When the Queen became pregnant, the King looked for company elsewhere."

Ursula gasped at the implication. Had she really played the part of a common whore? To be the King's mistress was the best many women could hope for, and indeed such a position came with rewards. Look at Bessie Blount, who was the daughter of a minor knight. The King's affection had won her family grants of land, and after the birth of Henry Fitzroy, Bessie was married off to someone previously beyond her reach. But Lady Anne had been the daughter of a duke and married to an earl. For her to stoop to such a thing was shameful.

"At first there was a misunderstanding about who her paramour had been, and angry words were exchanged between my husband and the man in question. If Lord Edward had known the truth, perhaps he would've been more circumspect." Lady Eleanor paused here to smile ruefully. They both knew it was not in her husband's nature to be politic once his temper was stoked. "As you can imagine, her husband wasn't thrilled to be a cuckold. She was sent packing and the King was angry with all of us. News of this spread all around the court and the King was ashamed to be spoken of like this. Even the Queen admonished him. It might just be rumours, but if she rebuked him, it was certainly the last time she did so."

"I understand," Ursula said.

Lady Eleanor, usually so cool and composed, gave a shake of her head and a cold smile spread across her lips. "You understand nothing, and I pray you will never be in a position where your honour is called into question. As women, our reputation is all we have, and it can disappear just like that." She snapped her fingers to emphasise her point. Then she sighed, settling down into her normal composure. "You aren't the first woman to dream of grandeur."

Ursula felt chastised.

"All this is also to say that while we are in France, you ought to be careful. We will not tolerate any whiff of scandal."

Tensing, Ursula straightened. "I know better than that."

"So did Anne."

Saying nothing further, Lady Eleanor became indifferent once more to her company.

The baggage carts were loaded and set off for Dover. Ursula and Lady Eleanor would be travelling with a retinue of guards and attendants. Her husband sent a courteous note saying he was pleased she would be coming on this voyage, and to give his son a kiss for him.

Ursula's desire for adventure was tempered by the bad roads. They stayed at the very best abbeys on their way, sleeping on feather beds, yet nothing could shake off the exhaustion of travel, or the dust of the road.

In no time at all she found herself longing for Penshurst, with all the comforts of home.

Along the way her mare threw a shoe. There wasn't time for a blacksmith to repair it, so she switched to an unfamiliar bay that required a firm hand on the reins lest it run wild.

At last she saw the first signs of Dover. Her heart lifted at the sight of banners and flags. It was clear to all that the nobility of England had gathered in this one place. There was an exuberant energy all around her as they rode through the streets until they found the Duke's household.

He'd been set up in a townhome. It was richly furnished and comfortable. Neither the Duke nor her husband were home when they arrived, and Ursula was not to be seen, with her travel-stained cloak and weary face.

She commanded the servants to bring her a bath, and spent the better part of the day scrubbing the grime from her body and soaking her sore muscles in the steaming hot water scented with thyme and fennel.

A maid pulled out a fresh gown from Ursula's chests, and by the time her husband arrived home there was no evidence of her exhaustion.

"It's been far too long," Henry said, coming forward to kiss her in greeting. "There has been so much to do. Sorry for not writing to you more; I'm glad to hear Henry is thriving in the nursery."

"I'm happy to see you looking so well too," Ursula replied. "When are we to set sail?"

"In a few days, if the weather holds. I told my father we should set off now. What's the point of delaying?"

Ursula's brow arched. Clearly, her husband would've been happy enough to leave with or without her.

"I am certain the King wishes everything to be just

right. There's no sense hurrying and making a mess of the whole thing."

Henry let out a guffaw. "The King has nothing to do with any of this. It's all Wolsey's planning. Knowing him, he's been ready for weeks but he's just as happy to have us dancing to his tune."

Ursula looked away lest he catch the irritation on her face. His complaints just made Wolsey sound like a competent minister.

"Your father has emptied his treasury of his jewels. It feels as though we've brought everything with us," Ursula said, switching the topic.

"It's no less than any other man of sense has done. There's a king's ransom in the city at this very moment. Everyone's trying to outdo each other with finery. I heard the Earl of Pembroke complain about a sore neck, and we all laughed. It's no wonder your neck is sore, I told him, and I pointed to the three large chains he wore about his shoulders. Not to mention his rings and fine embroidered jacket."

Ursula flinched, hoping her husband hadn't been quite so crass.

"The King is determined the English court outshines the French," he said.

"And there was I, thinking we were to be friends and that this meeting would finally put an end to all hostilities between us."

There was a twinkle of amusement in Henry's eyes as he regarded her. "That doesn't mean there shouldn't be some friendly competition between our two nations." Then he leaned in closer, grasping her hands in his. "When the crown of France is on our king's head and he regains his ancient rights, that's when we will finally get along with the French." He laughed at his own jest, and twirled her around as though they were dancing.

It was hard not to get caught up in his excitement, and before long Ursula found herself smiling.

"I am anxious to see my family. I know they are here too," Ursula said later that evening as they lay side by side in bed, her hair loose and sprawled across the pillow beneath her.

"Your mother is among the Queen's ladies and your brothers are in the King's household. It will be a merry family reunion."

"I long to see them. Will you take me?"

He looked perturbed. "I–I have duties to see to."

"I know, but—"

"When we land in France there will be plenty of time."

"Shall we not take the same ship across the Channel?" She'd been under the impression that as the Duke was the King's cousin, they would travel with him.

Henry's face was sour as he looked away. "It doesn't matter. Father has arranged for us to have comfortable lodgings and there's nothing to worry about. We will only be on the sea for a few hours."

Suddenly, she remembered her mother-in-law's warnings. "The King is not upset with you or your father, is he?" she asked, placing a hand on her husband's forearm to force him to look at her.

"It is none of your concern." His sharp tone revealed far more than his reassurances. Sensing he had revealed too much, Henry gave her a disarming smile and placed a chaste kiss on her temple. "There is nothing for you to worry about," he reiterated. "Leave everything to my father and me to manage. You are my beautiful bride and you shouldn't be troubled by a little foolishness."

Ursula pursed her lips, wondering whether to press the point further.

He tapped the tip of her nose with a finger. "I see you are quite determined to uncover every little secret. It's just a bit of trouble with Wolsey. Nothing new on that score, is there?" He winked, trying to make light of the situation, but Ursula felt uneasy.

Wolsey wasn't merely the King's favoured councillor, he was also a cardinal and the Papal Legate. Would it be so hard for him to bring down a mere duke if he wanted to? A shiver of fear coursed through her.

Her husband pulled the furs over her. "I shall let you rest now. Charles Brandon is hosting an evening of entertainment at his house."

"Enjoy yourself," Ursula said, watching him go. She wished she'd been able to persuade him to take her to see her mother. Margaret Pole was wise and astute; she would know which way the wind was blowing and would be able to give her advice.

Her husband and his family were eager to pretend they were untouchable and more powerful than the likes of Thomas Wolsey. However, Ursula's own family history told a different story. Her grandfather had been a duke and brother to the King of England. That didn't save him when the accusations of treason fell upon his shoulders. He died, drowned in a barrel of his favourite wine, or so the rumours said. Ursula had never been brave enough to ask her mother. Things hadn't improved when Henry VII took the throne. He'd been suspicious of all those with Plantagenet blood. Her uncle, Edward, imprisoned as a child in the Tower of London, had been beheaded on trumped-up charges. Her mother would pray for him and never failed to acknowledge the day of his death. Lady Margaret herself escaped the axe only because she was married into a small family of Tudor loyalists, but they were kept in poverty.

This king had been tender to his mother's cousin, and restored some of her wealth. But he could change his mind.

Ursula tried to shake off these dark thoughts, but found it impossible. They were like gnats swarming around her head. As she prepared to sleep that night, she said a special prayer to God to protect her small son, come what may.

CHAPTER 4

1520

A t the end of May they finally embarked.

The sky was a bright eggshell blue, and the breeze was just strong enough to fill the sails without turning the waters tumultuous. With no danger of capsizing or getting lost at sea, Ursula felt optimistic about the journey ahead.

Finding her sea legs quickly, she stood on the prow of the ship, keeping her eyes fixed on the horizon. Dover had been a flurry of activity and noise. She was glad they'd left.

"We will be able to see land soon," Henry said, coming up beside her. "The captain informed me it won't be long now."

Ursula nodded. Their ship was just behind King Henry's, and beautiful harp music was being carried on the wind towards them. For a moment she shut her eyes, listening to the soothing sound. They were surrounded on all sides by a flotilla of ships, all decked out finely to carry the six thousand members of the court and their attendants chosen to take part in this spectacular event.

The magnitude of this venture began to dawn on her.

Even at this late stage, not everything was ready. Ursula had five women in her quarters still working away at her gowns, making last-minute adjustments here and there.

The court would disembark at Calais and spend a few days in the fortified city while final preparations were being made. Then on the appointed day they would ride out to meet with King Francis's court.

It had been agreed the two parties would meet on neutral territory between Guînes and Ardres. Henry had shown her the location on a map. Now he placed a hand over hers on the rail of the ship. "Can you imagine all that land was once ours?"

At her arched eyebrow he amended it to, "England's." She had to laugh, because to her husband, that was one and the same as the Staffords.

"It's a pity the Crown wasn't able to hold on to France," he said, as if it had been a choice and something easily rectified.

"Well, if Princess Mary is betrothed to France, our two nations may one day unite. Her children would rule over both France and England. Perhaps even Scotland too."

Henry turned to her with a scowl. "We would never accept a French king."

Ursula, swayed by the sea, was indifferent to his disgust. "Sometimes it's easier to accept the way things are than to fight against the tide. Combined, our two great nations would rival any other."

"That is a woman's answer to everything." He shook his head. "We would never capitulate to such a solution."

"A pity," Ursula murmured under her breath. Her

words were carried off by the wind and he didn't hear her. He was right — they would never see eye to eye, but their gender had nothing to do with it.

"The King may yet have a son by the Queen, and if not then he could always have Fitzroy legitimised," Henry said, for once curbing his tongue from naming his other great hope.

"That would plunge England into civil war. There aren't many who would accept a bastard on England's throne."

"Yes, exactly," Henry said, as though the thought was thrilling.

Ursula wondered if her husband was a fool, or merely ambitious. But not wishing to discover the truth of it she excused herself, saying she wasn't feeling well.

As their ship docked at Calais, they were greeted by a crowd of cheering onlookers. The King and Queen had already disembarked, and they progressed through the streets to great rejoicing by the people.

Ursula wished she'd been able to catch sight of them as they rode with their large retinue towards Stable Inn. Henry had told her it would accommodate two thousand people. It was hard to imagine the grand scale of such an inn. 'Palace' would surely have been a more suitable name.

Now that their own ship had docked, they prepared to make the journey to the castle, where the Duke of Buckingham had arranged accommodations for the whole family.

"We'll be far more comfortable there. Baron Lisle is of our affinity. We couldn't trust the likes of Wolsey to understand what we expect as great lords of England," Henry said, as they stood together while the grooms led their horses down the gangplank.

"I have no doubt about Lord Lisle's warm welcome. I was merely curious as to why the King wouldn't give your father rooms closer to his own."

Henry shrugged. "He doesn't want to be eclipsed by us."

Or he was showing the world they weren't favoured. But Ursula kept that to herself. Her mother would be lodged near the Queen. Perhaps she'd be able to visit her.

Ursula's maid came forward. "My lady, we've unpacked your cloak for the journey. Do you wish to refresh yourself?"

Happy for an excuse to leave, Ursula nodded and retreated to her private room.

She touched the cloak's soft fabric, marvelling at the intricate embroidery and fine quality of the material. Her maids would have to carry the train until she mounted her horse. It would look dazzling with the bright sun overhead.

Indeed, this was the reason why the population of Calais had turned out to watch the arrival of the King of England and his retinue. With each noble trying to outdo the other, they created an amazing spectacle no one wished to miss.

At last they were mounted on their horses. Ursula's cloak draped elegantly around her as she sat erect in the saddle. Her husband rode ahead at his father's side. Both men were decked in cream-coloured doublets with heavy gold chains about their necks. She admired how Henry carried himself. He sat tall in the saddle and looked confident as he glanced around. They would be at the forefront of the cavalcade.

A retinue of guards richly dressed in Buckingham livery would protect them as they made their way through the crowded streets.

As they set out to a blast of trumpets, Henry's expression eased and he had a smile ready for anyone who cheered. The very picture of a gracious prince, Ursula envied his confidence.

Her attention was pulled away by a commotion to her left. She was forced to rein in her horse as someone charged forward to hand her a posy of flowers. Seeing no threat, Ursula called to the guards to let her through and she smiled graciously at the young woman as she accepted the flowers.

She looked over at her mother-in-law riding beside her; she nodded approvingly at how Ursula had handled herself.

Everyone from the servants to the Duke was dressed in the azure blue and the red of the Buckingham coat of arms. Ursula's fine cream brocade cloak was woven with strands of shimmering gold thread. Her maids had spent an entire week cleverly affixing a crimson chevron made of silk so that the point rested at the base of her neck. To add further contrast, the edges were elegantly adorned with red squirrel fur, and to fasten it, she had selected a magnificent ruby brooch.

In such finery she felt resplendent, but she disappeared into the background next to Lady Eleanor. Her mother-in-law had chosen a blue azure cloak over a silver tissue dress. It was embroidered with lions and fleur-de-lis in silver thread and trimmed with white fur. The ensemble created a dazzling display of wealth and prestige; she looked ethereal. How did she do it? Was it the soft expression that smoothed the lines on her face, or the graceful flick of her wrist as she acknowledged those who called out to her? Everyone who beheld her knew this was a great lady of the realm.

Ursula was envious, for although she had been brought up as a proper gentlewoman, with all the training her position in life required of her, she had been kept in the country. The pomp and ceremony of public functions was still new to her, and it wasn't long before she felt the strain of the effort and uncertainty catching up to her.

Occasionally, she heard the clink of coins being thrown to the crowd by their servants, which only intensified the cheering.

At the castle gates, Arthur Plantagenet, the Lord Deputy of Calais, waited. He was a middle-aged man with none of the rumoured beauty of his family. But he was a gracious host and eagerly brought them inside, away from the crowds and heat of the day.

"Everything has been prepared for your stay," Arthur said, clasping the Duke of Buckingham's arms. "It's been a long time since you've graced the city with your presence."

"Far too long," Edward Stafford said. "But I see you are looking well."

Arthur gave a hearty laugh, patting his belly. "If by that you mean I've grown rounder, then you'd be right. I'm no longer the fit young man I was before, but I'm wiser for it."

The Duke scoffed and allowed himself to be led through the gallery to the stone staircase beyond.

Arthur showed them to their rooms himself. Ursula was pleased to find hers was well stocked with everything she could possibly need, including a tray laden with sweet-meats, hard cheese and bread.

From the narrow slit window she could make out the sea, where gulls were darting about.

"There is a banquet tonight at the Stable Inn," Henry said, appearing suddenly her room.

Ursula blinked at the unexpected intrusion. They'd lived apart for so long she was no longer used to his presence.

"Are we invited to attend?" she asked, not wishing to assume. Really, she should have him sit down with her to explain in detail what was going to happen. She hated surprises and being ill prepared. The least he could do was let her know what to expect.

"My father's going. I don't know if I shall bother," he said, as petulant as a child — which meant he hadn't been expressly invited and his pride was injured.

Feeling tender towards him, she ran her hands over the fitted sleeves of his jacket. "What is more important is that we're here, and that we'll be at the meeting between the two kings. This will be a monumental occasion, one that won't soon be forgotten."

He leaned his forehead against hers and breathed in deep. She was glad she'd perfumed her hair with rosemary water that morning.

"You are right. In the procession my father will be given the place of honour and I will be right behind him."

"You see, the King hasn't forgotten about you." She moved back to the window. "Besides, Stable Inn will be chaotic today. Everyone is still settling in. I would wager it's far more comfortable here. Lord Arthur has been so kind."

Henry scoffed. "As he should be. My father has always supported him. And we are family, after all."

She nodded, though she hated it when he took on that imperious tone, as if he was owed the world. He wasn't, but there was no point arguing with him.

They retired for the evening not long after, heading to their separate chambers. The following day Ursula heard that Henry had gone out roistering in the taverns of Calais. She tried her best not to be irritated with him, but the moment he complained of a headache she shot him a look that told him he deserved far more.

On the third night in Calais, the whole family visited the King's court at Stable Inn. It was Ursula's first time at court since she was a child, and she was giddy with excitement.

They entered the large hall, which was beautifully decorated with banners painted with Tudor roses. The King and Queen sat together beneath the canopy of estate, with the hated Wolsey sitting not far away.

Ursula followed on the Duke's heels as he approached the dais to make his bow. She'd chosen a deep green gown with slashed sleeves that allowed the silver linen shift beneath to show through. She dripped with emeralds, from her embroidered petticoat to her headdress. Looking around she was happy to find she was neither overdressed nor underdressed. Many watched her progress towards the royal couple.

The King was magnanimous as he waved for them to approach. "I am glad to see you in such high spirits," he said, eyeing the Duke carefully. "How are the Marches? Has the unrest been quelled?"

"Yes, Your Majesty." The Duke's expression was pinched with displeasure at being reminded of the public rebuke he received from the King just a few months ago.

Ursula's gaze moved to the Queen. When she'd first come to her throne she'd been known as a great beauty. Now, beside her husband, the age difference between them was clear. He was handsome and strong while she looked wan and compliant. She was plump to his athletic physique. A stranger arriving at court for the first time might have been surprised to learn that Henry had once loved her ardently, and married her against the wishes of his grandmother.

As Ursula's mother had served the Queen for so many years, she was aware of all the sorrows Katherine had suffered. She wore the loss of each child in the deep grooves on her face. The hair peeking out from beneath her English hood was streaked with grey.

Yet for all of this she was the Queen, and no one could find fault with her composure.

"Lady Ursula," she said, catching her eye. "Come forward."

Ursula did so, curtseying low until she was bid to rise.

"The last time I saw you, you were just a child. Now look at how you've grown, and married too."

"Yes, Your Majesty."

The Queen smiled benevolently.

"With a son in the cradle already," the Duke of Buckingham interjected.

Ursula flushed at his remark.

"I heard. Congratulations, my dear. May God bless you with many more fine children."

"Thank you, Your Majesty." Ursula bobbed up and down again. Her eyes scanned the crowd; she wished she could disappear from sight. The Queen made no indication that the Duke's bragging affected her, but Ursula could only imagine how she felt. Every other woman it seemed was able to give their husband a living son. Yet she had failed.

"You will be searching for your mother," Queen Katherine said with a knowing smile. "She is with your brother Montagu, over there. You may go and greet them."

Ursula thanked her. "You are very kind. It's been a long time since I last saw her. Excuse me, Your Majesty." And she left, but not before bowing to the King as well.

She moved expertly through the crowded hall until she found her mother and brother, deep in conversation.

"Ursula!" Margaret held out her hands and they embraced. "I had hoped to see you before now. My, how well you look." She beamed. "And that gown suits you."

"*Merci*," Ursula said, switching to French. She gave a tiny twirl so her mother might see the beautiful embroidery to its full effect. "I hope I shall give no cause to embarrass my husband."

Her mother tutted. "Ridiculous. I don't need to remind you of your own lineage. You've been raised to be a great lady and I expect you to hold yourself as one. But come, sit by my side, if your husband can spare you. I need you to tell me all about my little grandson."

"Of course, I'd love to," Ursula said, taking a moment to smile at her oldest brother. "And you must tell me your news. I heard Jane is with child too. Congratulations."

He bowed his head. "She wished she could come but she was too far along."

"I'm sure you will find the time to write to her about all the little details, and a small gift would go a long way to smoothing over any resentment," Ursula said.

He grinned. "You've grown wise, sister."

"With Reginald gone from home, someone has to be. Who else would advise you all on how to conduct your affairs?" she joked, and her mother tutted again.

When it was time to retire, Ursula's throat was sore from all the conversation. Her husband had invited her to dance and she was proud of how well she had conducted herself. Now, back in her chamber, her maids carefully removed layer after layer of finery, massaged lavender oil on her brows and combed out her long hair. After braiding it into long plaits she climbed onto the feather bed and fell into a deep slumber.

The celebrations continued on. Every day there was something new to do, and yet anticipation was mounting as the day of their departure to meet the French king approached.

"Father will be at the forefront of the procession," Henry said, as they broke their fast together. "The Duke of Suffolk will be there as well. We will be somewhere further back. I wish I had some title of my own."

"Too late to worry about that now. No one who sees you will doubt you are anything but a great man of noble heritage."

Her husband's frown lessened, but didn't disappear completely.

"Your brother, Arthur, was knighted," he said. "I should've gone to France too."

"You were fourteen at the time. Arthur was twenty. You cannot compare yourself to him."

These days she found she was constantly finding ways to smooth over his insecurities. Ursula knew it was just the anxiety of this momentous event.

"Will you be riding in the lists?"

"Father doesn't think it's a good idea, but the King is taking part and he doesn't even have a son! I will not look like a coward by not participating."

Spoken like a spoiled prince. However, for once Ursula was sympathetic.

Her husband was increasingly frustrated with the lack of responsibility and control he had over his own life. He was far past the age of needing to rely on his father. But beyond being given the courtesy title of Earl of Stafford, he was still a part of his father's household. By contrast, Ursula's mother had heaped responsibility on her eldest son and heir, trying to encourage his independence. It was a shame the Duke didn't see fit to do the same.

Now, his father forbidding him from riding in the lists was just another insult. Ursula knew he was capable. She'd seen him practicing at the tiltyard back in England. He had impeccable training, but there was always an edge of fear in him as he rode towards his opponent. That fear often caused him to make a mistake and lose.

Now Ursula was fearful that the more his father refused to give him autonomy, the more his confidence would be worn down. Would her husband be suffocated beneath his father's overbearing authority?

"Henry, you must do as you please. Ride in the jousts and win the day. I'm sure you will," she said, leaning across the table to place a kiss on his brow. "I've never seen such a good rider before."

He grimaced. "Now you are just trying to flatter me into silence."

"If you put your mind to it I doubt anyone could stand in your way." She laughed. "As for your accusation, you are wrong. I would like you to have something to occupy your time so I might have a respite from your attention."

Indeed, if he wasn't riding out with his friends he was pulling her to bed. She didn't mind so much, and the thought that she might have another child pleased her. Little Harry should have lots of playmates.

"I don't recall you complaining the other night," he said, making her cheeks flush.

S even days after arriving, they prepared at last to travel towards the Val d'Or. Organising the large procession would have been an undertaking beyond the power of most men, but Wolsey and his officials arranged everything to perfection, down to the smallest detail.

As a result there was no jostling for position between the nobles as they found their place in line. The English court was a glamourous streak of gold and silver weaving through the streets of Calais.

Anticipation mounted as they waited for the signal to start out. Even Ursula's mare, usually so calm, pulled against her reins.

When the trumpets blared, Ursula's breath caught.

The procession was slow but aided by the sound of drums and trumpets announcing to all their arrival.

The King had brought with him five hundred Yeomen of the Guard, dressed in resplendent crimson. Kites flew high in the air and banners were carried aloft by strong men. Far and wide, all would know Henry Tudor was on the march.

Ursula took a look behind her at the long line of courtiers and the servants bringing up the rear. Some were on foot and some mounted on fine horses, but not a single one could be called dowdy. Eager to make an impression, the King had ordered that everyone from the lowliest kitchen boy to the highest duke should be well dressed. It must have cost a fortune to kit the servants out with their new uniforms of red and gold.

Her husband rode ahead with his father once again. Often he looked over his shoulder to check on her. Occasionally, they shared a secret smile. His newfound attentiveness warmed her to the core, and she was hopeful that in time they would grow closer still. She doubted they would ever come to passionately love each other, but the thought of him asking for her opinion and valuing it pleased her.

As they neared Ardres, the English trumpeters heard a responding call. Squinting against the sun, Ursula tried to catch sight of the French court. They were a mere blip on the horizon. She couldn't make anything out and had to remind herself not to lean forward in the saddle like an excitable child.

The procession slowed to a near halt up ahead. Ursula heard the heralds and then another blast of trumpets.

Something was wrong. The French had halted, but Ursula couldn't see why. For the briefest moment she feared this could be a trap — they were on enemy territory, after all, and the French were known to resort to such treachery.

But then King Henry broke away from his court and

rode towards King Francis. When the person in front of her shifted, Ursula caught a glimpse of the Kings doffing their caps and then dismounting in what seemed like practiced unison.

A great cheer went up all around her, and she supposed they embraced. The people who'd arranged this meeting were surely breathing a sigh of relief.

With the formal greetings over, the courtiers began to dismount. Ursula finally took in the magnificence around her. Tents and pavilions were set up all around. Cloth of gold appeared to cover every surface and at the centre of it all was a timber palace with a false facade of stonework.

"Magnificent, is it not?" Henry pulled up beside her. He jumped down from his horse and then helped her slide from her own saddle.

"I've never seen such a sight. I feel as though I'm in a dream." The panels of fabric were arranged to complete the illusion this was a small walled city. Touching one of the panels, Ursula was surprised to find it was real silk.

"There's more treasure here than in El Dorado," Henry said, a huge grin on his face. He glanced around and then stole a quick kiss.

"I will see you situated with my mother, and then I must return to my father's side," he said, taking her by the elbow.

Grooms were already leading the horses away. Ursula wondered where they'd all be stabled, but there was so much to distract her she quickly forgot about them.

The Duke's tents were clustered together in the semblance of a small private manor. A prowling lion holding the Buckingham Banners in its paw distinguished it from the others.

As they approached, a servant pulled aside the opening to let them through. Ursula stepped inside a small paradise. Carpets in shades of red and green covered the floor with heavy panels used to divide up the tent into smaller rooms. A servant came forward to take their cloaks. As Ursula warmed her hands on the brazier, she glanced around at the tables and chairs arranged about the room. The duke was prepared to entertain a large number of people.

After they drank some ale, they explored their rooms. Ursula was pleased to find a feather bed waiting for her. As she stepped on the carpets, the air filled with the spicy scent of cloves and cinnamon. The servants had taken care to dust the carpets with a perfumed powder. She also noted the pomanders hanging from chains along the sides of the tent. While it might appear excessive, it wouldn't be long before the unpleasant odours of hundreds of people living in close quarters would permeate through the tent walls.

"A paradise on Earth," Henry said, with a heavy sigh. "Are you pleased?"

She nodded, feeling elated even as the exhaustion was catching up to her.

Guessing her thoughts, he smiled and said, "We have endless entertainments ahead of us. Take a moment to rest while I go speak to my father."

Left to her own devices, Ursula put aside her urge to explore and concentrated on more practical matters. Not knowing when there would be time to eat, she requested some food, and water to wash with. Depending on the day, her gown would have to be changed at least two or three times.

As her maid laid out a fresh gown for her, Ursula touched the brilliant cream silk. The French ladies had worn plain gowns in dark colours, yet they were alluring in their simplicity and made her own choices feel gaudy. When her maid offered to bring out her jewel box, she refused. Her wedding ring and small gold cross would suffice.

The Field of the Cloth of Gold, as it was being referred to, never ceased to amaze. Near the temporary wood palace was a fountain that spouted wine.

Henry dipped his goblet into it and brought it away laughing. "We must have something like this installed at Penshurst," he said, stumbling.

"My lord, we shall do no such thing," Ursula said, steadying herself as he bumped into her.

"Why ever not? I am to be the duke! Whatever I say goes." He ended his little tirade with a hiccup that sent him laughing.

"And nothing shall ever get done."

"What are you saying?"

She nudged him, and he stumbled forward. "If you had access to free-flowing wine not only would our treasury be depleted, but you'd be too drunk to notice."

He chuckled. "I'm sure I'd notice. Once the fountain ran dry."

"You are incorrigible. What would your father say if he saw you now?"

Henry shrugged, and seeing he was more far gone than he should have been, she pulled him back towards their tent, determined to put him in his bed and ensure he didn't do anything that would embarrass the family.

He wasn't the only nobleman teetering on the edge of foolishness. None of this was a surprise. With a never-ending stream of wine, music and fine food, an air of frivolity had overtaken them all. The smallest part of her longed for the quiet of Penshurst.

Once inside their tent, Ursula pushed him down on a cushioned seat. She summoned his valet with a snap of her fingers and set about helping him undress her hapless husband.

"Did you know the French thought we'd come armed?"

Her eyes snapped to Henry's face; she wondered if he was joking.

He nodded gravely. "They saw the glint of all our riches and thought we were an army coming to attack them. Imagine that — you, wielding a sword." He chucked her under her chin and she shook him off.

She grimaced as she fought with the laces of his boots.

"Husband, you shall have to learn to hold your drink if you are ever to become a duke."

Henry seemed to find this very amusing. His arms shot out and he would've fallen backwards had it not been for the return of the valet.

Ursula stood, reaching the end of her patience. She turned to the valet and said, "Put him to bed. Make sure he has plenty of water and nothing else to drink. He will prob- ably be sick as a dog in the morning."

"Yes, my lady." The valet bowed.

She retreated with her own lady, determined to enjoy what was left of the evening—she'd see if she could find her family.

Her mother's tent was close to the temporary palace, distinguished by the coat of arms of Plantagenet lions and the Warwick eagle and the ragged staff stitched into the side of the tents and banners.

Recognising Ursula, the servant poked his head through the tent entrance to announce her arrival.

"Ursula, step inside," her mother urged. "What are you doing wandering about at night?"

"My husband has been put to bed and I felt the need to get away from the stench of alcohol."

Her mother pursed her lips but invited her to sit.

"How is the Queen?" Ursula asked, noticing immedi- ately the withdrawn look in her mother's eye.

"Tired, God bless her. The last few days have been trying for her. King Francis doesn't miss a single chance to flaunt his two sons before the King, and Henry turns that anger onto the Queen." Margaret gave a shake of her head.

It wasn't fair that women were blamed for not bearing sons. The King had been kind in the past and careful of his wife's feelings. Now he was more than happy to scold her in public for her failure. Queen Katherine bore his insults with dignity, but it was hard for her.

"Now that the peace treaty is signed, we can enjoy the feasts and tournaments. Perhaps it will put the King in a good mood," Margaret said, rubbing at her temples.

Ursula reached for her mother. "Is there anything I can do to help you?"

"Seeing you is doing me a world of good already."

The unexpected loving comment from her mother unnerved Ursula. "I hear there will be a ceremony tomorrow in which the queens will greet each other."

"That is true. A formal banquet has been arranged and I'm sure there will be all sorts of spectacular displays of wealth and entertainment. Everyone is eager to outdo one another."

"You don't approve?"

Margaret shrugged. "It feels as though this is all an empty show. If there was true love between our nations, then we wouldn't have met with Emperor Charles before setting off for France. The French have accused us of playing a double game, and perhaps we are. It'd be a shame if we spent all this time and money on this treaty only for us to become enemies once again."

"Well, war brings with it the chance of glory. My own brothers were knighted on the field of battle."

Her mother shook her head. "Don't long for war. Thérouanne was a petty skirmish. A true war would bring destruction and sadness to both sides, even if we came out victorious. Come now, it's not correct for us to be discussing war when we are here for peace talks."

"Is it true you've found Arthur a bride?" Ursula asked, thinking of the teasing comment her brother Henry had made when they dined together in Dover.

"Oh yes," Margaret said, leaning back in her chair. "Another Jane. She's the daughter of Sir Roger Lewkenor and Lord Barentyne's widow. Perhaps, not a brilliant marriage but she is an heiress."

"Is she pretty?"

Her mother's face scrunched up, as if the matter was unimportant, but at last she nodded. "I believe they will get along well. She comes from a good family." Which meant they were an ancient family rooted in old traditions, and didn't embrace the new teachings. Would Jane even be literate? Ursula kept the question to herself. Her mother believed that too much education was bad for women, and that beyond learning a bit of Latin in order to read the Bible, girls had no business being in the schoolroom.

Ursula had always found this ironic, as her mother had become a countess in her own right and thus yielded as much power as an earl. Even as a child, Ursula was given a far more modern education — something her mother claimed she didn't approve of. Luckily, now Ursula was married, she had escaped from her mother's censure and could freely read whatever she wanted to at Penshurst. The library there was excellent and her husband was always buying new books. Henry thought it was fashionable to have such a well-read wife, and encouraged her.

"We haven't had much time alone, so I want to ask now if all is at it should be?" Her mother spoke in a whisper. "The Duke isn't depriving you of anything? Has your allowance been paid out quarterly?"

Ursula's cheeks felt hot. "No. I am given everything I could possibly want."

Her mother let out a sigh of relief. "Good." She leaned back in her seat. "I know the Duke is an honest man, but promises can be broken or forgotten with time. It's why I ensure everything promise is made legally binding with contracts."

"You'd sue the Duke over my marriage contract?" Ursula asked, incredulous. Her mother had never exactly been tender to her. She'd been kind, and attentive to her education, but love was reserved for her son and heir, Henry.

"I would," her mother said, stoutly. "It would be a matter of principle and I would not like to see my only daughter beggared."

Grinning, Ursula looked down at her gown. The cream silk embroidered with roses in silver thread was hardly what she imagined a beggar would wear.

"Tomorrow, after the queens meet, we will enjoy the first of many jousts. I would like you to be by my side," Margaret said, entwining her fingers together. "I wish your father-in-law saw fit to bring you to court. It's the only way you can help your family rise in favour."

"Serving the Queen doesn't seem to carry much favour with the King these days. Everyone comments on her... failure to produce an heir. They compare her to Queen Claude who is young and beautiful, with two sons and another child on the way. It's hard not to wonder why Queen Katherine has only one daughter."

"It is God's will. Who can question it?" her mother hissed. "Queen Katherine is a devout woman."

Ursula looked away, sorry she had even broached the subject. Her mother was tender to the former Spanish princess under her guardianship. There was no point in saying that the Queen's influence had been waning for some time and that if her mother wished to ingratiate herself with the King then she should look elsewhere.

"Have you heard from Reginald?" Ursula asked, wishing to change the topic.

Her mother took a moment to answer. "He is still in Padua but he often travels to other countries. The Pope has taken notice of him. Imagine that. My scholarly son." She beamed, ignoring the fact that many of her children were studious. They, however, had not been given a choice in the matter. Long before they were old enough to understand, their paths had been decided for them. Ursula was merely grateful her mother had sought such a good match for her. Poor Geoffrey, the youngest, faced the most difficult road. He had neither the Church nor a degree to fall back on. Their mother would be generous and give him a manor or two, but she wouldn't wish to divide up Henry's inheritance.

As the fourth and final child, two years younger than Ursula, he had been spoiled, but was now finding that being born last meant slim pickings when it came to favours and fortune. His brothers had been found places at court, but he was raised at home in the country, as Ursula had been. She knew it wouldn't be long before the reality of this hit him. Would he still be able to strut around in luxurious clothing, and gamble without a care in the world? Perhaps their mother would find him an heiress to marry. She certainly had a knack for finding them.

Before long Ursula retired to her own tent, thanking her mother for the invitation to sit in the Queen's box with her.

Lady Eleanor was just returning as well, and Ursula curtseyed to her mother-in-law.

"Good evening, Lady Eleanor."

Her eyes studied her coolly. "Where have you been?"

"Visiting my mother. She's told me tomorrow there is to be a tournament—"

"Yes. The Duke has been appointed as one of the judges."

"Will Henry take part? I know it is his greatest wish to demonstrate his valour to the French."

Lady Eleanor's eyes were hard and she gave a slight shake of her head. "It's out of the question."

"Why?" Ursula wasn't sure why she was daring to challenge her. Many assumed that Lady Eleanor was a passive observer, when, in fact, she was a force to be reckoned with. The Duke allowed her to have far more influence than anyone realised.

"You should know why. He's my only son." A treasure to be protected. "Jousting is a dangerous sport. If he is itching for a fight, there's plenty to do in the Welsh Marches. Indeed, he will be called upon to do just that shortly. Enough of this — he should be grateful he was allowed to come to France at all." She strode away, leaving Ursula taken aback.

She knew she should set the matter aside, but she was stubborn too.

Ursula had seen a joust or two in her life, but never on a scale such as this. There were three anointed queens in attendance: Queen Katherine of England, Queen Claude of France, and the Dowager Queen Mary of France.

Each had their own pavilion decorated with rich fabrics and tapestries. The ladies accompanying them were so numerous that many had to watch from carts or their palfreys.

Ursula was grateful her mother had obtained her a seat in Queen Katherine's box. Before the tournament began, acrobats and fire eaters entertained the crowd. An impressive display of fireworks put an end to the frivolity and the combatants took to the field. Everyone cheered as the English and French knights took turns parading around the enclosure.

Everywhere she turned there was something new to see; monkeys juggling, dogs walking on their hindquarters balancing little balls on their noses. Ursula tried to take it all in.

Then the real tournament began.

Queen Katherine applauded as King Henry arrived on the field in a full suit of armour. He saluted the crowd and then his fellow monarch, who would be battling on the same side.

The judges were seated opposite the queens, and Ursula caught a glimpse of her husband standing at the ready behind the Duke of Buckingham. She hoped he had put aside his disappointment and would enjoy watching the jousting.

Wolsey stood, and the crowd fell silent as he said a blessing and a prayer over the congregation.

Then the first contenders were announced and took their positions on opposite ends of the ring.

Ursula watched the way the Queen gripped the armrests whenever the King took to the field. The moment it was over she jumped to her feet, applauding her valiant husband as if she had never had any doubt.

It was easy to be seriously injured while jousting. Horses could flounder; a lance might hit in just the wrong spot. It was not unheard of for participants to die.

Even though the two kings were on the same team, they tried to find ways to surpass the other, whether by scoring more points or being more daring. It certainly made for an exciting spectacle.

At one point King Francis took a hit to the face. His visor protected him, but his nose bled and although he won, he was escorted off the field shortly after.

As the joust came to a dramatic end, Ursula was finally able to breathe.

The English king was resplendent in his shining armour, triumphant after a day of hard-won matches and competitions. No one could say that either monarch had been up against opponents who let them win. They'd all fought hard.

Queen Katherine put a hand to her belly and Ursula's mother motioned for another lady to come forward with a tisane. Queen Katherine thanked her and smiled at her kindly.

Ursula didn't recognise the young woman, but she was very charming, with blonde hair and stunning eyes.

Now the queens each stood and in a choreographed move left their pavilions and met in the centre. Queen Claude and Queen Katherine embraced each other, before turning to embrace the Dowager Queen Mary too.

Ursula was too far away to hear what was being said, but she couldn't help but think that as exquisitely dressed as Queen Katherine was, she was eclipsed.

As the ladies of the three parties mingled, Ursula caught sight of the blonde woman from before, embracing a dark-haired French lady.

"The Boleyn sisters," her mother said, following the direction of her gaze. "Their father, Sir Thomas Boleyn, has been rising in the King's favour."

"Ah. I was wondering who she could be. I had no idea Thomas Boleyn was so well regarded." She paused, remembering how high handed she had acted towards him at Penshurst. In the future she would be more careful before giving offense. "Still, it's a wonder that the daughter of a mere knight is given such preference at an event. Then again, Cardinal Wolsey was also lowborn and look how high he has risen."

Her mother nodded. "The one who serves Queen Katherine is called Mary. Recently, she married William Carey, who rode in the lists today. The match is a good one for both sides. She is a sweet, biddable girl. Unlike others, she doesn't give the Queen any trouble and in turn, Her Majesty dotes on her."

"And the other?" Ursula took in the lady talking animatedly. Her dark eyes darted about and she was quick to smile at a passerby. One would never have guessed she was the younger sister from the dignified way she carried herself.

Her mother's brow furrowed as she tried to remember. "Anne, I believe. Their mother is the Duke of Norfolk's daughter, so they are not entirely without good connections. I overheard the King telling the Queen about Thomas Boleyn's claim on the earldom of Ormond. There are two claimants for that title and there are hopes it'll be solved through marriage. But come away now, I wish to rest before the banquet."

Just then Katherine, her sister-in-law and the new Countess of Westmorland, hurried by.

"Lady Katherine!" Ursula called out, unable to help herself. She hadn't seen her sister-in-law since her marriage.

Katherine stopped in her tracks and turned to her with a beaming smile. "Lady Ursula, I knew you had come." She curtseyed. "I was just going to find my sister. You have yet to meet her, why don't you join me and I'll introduce you?"

With her mother's blessing, she allowed Katherine to lead her away.

Elizabeth appeared to be about Ursula's age and was finely dressed in a cream gown edged with a band of azure velvet studded with precious gems.

"Sister, I thought I'd introduce you at last to our brother's wife. Elizabeth, this is Lady Ursula."

Lady Elizabeth bobbed a measured curtsey to them both before her eyes flew to Ursula's. This was Henry's oldest sister. Now that Ursula got a closer look at her features, she could see the family resemblance. She studied her clothes before settling her attention on her French hood, paired with a matching blue veil. Ursula couldn't help feeling a twinge of envy at the sight of it.

"It's a pleasure to meet you, Lady Ursula. I've heard a lot about you," she said, though thankfully without the sense of superiority that Ursula might have anticipated from this fashionable woman.

Something caught Katherine's eye. "I shall let you get acquainted, the Queen needs me." And off she went.

"So here we are," Lady Elizabeth said, eyeing Ursula up and down as though trying to get the measure of her. "The two duchesses-in-waiting." A grin split her serene features, and Ursula found herself smiling too.

"We are also sisters by marriage," Ursula pointed out. "It's a shame we haven't had the chance to meet until now."

"My husband, the Earl of Surrey, keeps me busy enough. I was married four years before you. Most of the time I live at Kenilworth Castle, you must come visit me," she said, taking Ursula's arm and leading her around a group of ladies towards the palace. "I have three children already, two sons and a daughter. For all that my husband seems content to please himself with other women."

Ursula couldn't keep the shock from her expression at such open talk.

Elizabeth shrugged. "If my husband is brazen about his affairs, why should I pretend not to know? I am determined not to be the sort of wife that turns a blind eye to her husband's indiscretions."

Ursula bit the inside of her cheek and looked around, scared her mother would overhear. Such blindness was often required of wives. Didn't the Queen herself put up with Bessie Blount for so long? And who knew who the King would choose as his next mistress.

As for Elizabeth's husband, the Earl of Surrey, she'd seen him riding in the lists but had yet to meet him in person. Unlike his aged father, he was imposing, and there had been something harsh in his features as he saluted the Queen of England. Maybe it was his imperious manner that didn't sit well with Ursula. It was surprising to find he had so much pride, bearing in mind his father, the Duke of Norfolk, had been a supporter of the Yorkists. When the first Henry Tudor took the crown, he and his family had been under suspicion. Much like her own mother, he had suffered under Henry VII's rule. Luckily, the current King Henry had been happy to let bygones be bygones and restored the family to their natural titles. Henry was, after all, the prince of both Lancaster and York.

Not wishing to offend, she settled on a safer topic. "My own son is barely a year old."

"I heard. My mother wrote me a long letter praising how beautiful and wise he already looked."

A laugh escaped Ursula. She couldn't imagine her mother-in-law doing so. "Did she really?"

"I'm sure I have kept the letter somewhere. I can show it to you sometime." Elizabeth shook her head ruefully. "From your surprise I take it my mother is still a block of ice." She grinned. "I can see I shock you with my forthright speech." She patted Ursula's hand. "You'll get used to it."

"I will?"

"Yes. I intend for us to be great friends, and to that effect you must have Henry bring you to court. You can't allow yourself to be tucked away in the country like some ornament in storage."

Ursula gaped. "Well, Henry himself is rarely at court."

"And that must change too." Elizabeth sighed. "It is tragic how we women are married into other families and thus separated from our loved ones."

By the end of their conversation, Ursula was certain she wished to see more of this determined woman. Elizabeth could clearly be abrasive and enjoyed shocking those around her, but she was entertaining and honest.

Elizabeth considered her for a moment and then said, "My sister looks happy in her new marriage."

"She does indeed," Ursula said, remembering the apprehension Katherine had felt at the prospect of marrying the Earl of Westmorland.

"I hope Ralph Neville treasures her as much as I do." Elizabeth's eyes flicked to Ursula's. "You must know by now, he wished to marry me but my heart was already set on another. He was young and I imagine he fancied himself in love with me. I doubt it was real."

"I'm sure you are right," Ursula said, her brows furrowed.

"Then I hope you will speak to her for me. She has not

visited me since her wedding and my letters go unanswered. She promised to spend time with me today but then weaselled her way out of it. I hope it doesn't continue. I am grateful this venture has given us the chance to be together again and perhaps, mend our relationship."

Ursula understood Elizabeth's dilemma now. Her heart went out to her. "I shall do what I can."

"Thank you," Elizabeth said.

Later that evening Ursula returned to her mother's side, ready to help as they accompanied the Queen back to her apartments.

With women fussing all around, it was hard not to notice the bland look in the Queen's eye. Nothing seemed to entice her or make her smile.

"The Queen is melancholic," Ursula remarked under her breath, watching her mother's shoulders slump.

"She misses her daughter, and it pains her to be reminded that she has only one child."

Queen Claude's belly had been on display during the tournament, and she made a great show of stroking it. To her credit she was likely not doing it to rub it in Queen Katherine's face. Ursula remembered how uncomfortable she had been as her pregnancy had advanced and Henry kicked her incessantly.

"The moments they have together grow less frequent, and soon a great marriage will be arranged for the Princess."

"To France?" Ursula asked, curious, given her mother's ambiguity.

Her mother shrugged. "It's too early to tell. But I have sworn to accompany her wherever she goes, to see that she is settled in her new home."

"But —" Ursula bit her tongue, stopping short of calling her mother old. She'd been speaking truthfully, earlier, about admiring her mother's dedication to the Crown, but resentment still lingered. As a child she had longed for her mother, who was either busy serving the Queen or helping to raise the Princess. However, this wasn't uncommon. It was the fate of all noble children to be raised by others, or fostered out into other households so alliances might be made.

"I won't need to go for several years. The princess is too young and precious to her father for him to send her away so quickly." What was left unsaid was that for now, she was his only heir. However, this also increased her value in marriage tenfold – the prospect of inheriting England was a tempting prospect.

Back in her own tent, Ursula's maids undressed her. Then she busied herself washing away the dust of the tournament.

Towards the end, the weather had shifted and gusts of wind brought a temporary halt to the proceedings. There was to be a banquet to mark the first day of festivities, and she would change into something fresh. Having scrubbed herself clean, she removed her old shift and sent it to be washed by the laundress.

Deciding to mimic the French fashions, she chose one of her simpler gowns. The red crimson petticoat added colour to her cheeks, and she selected a simple gold chain to adorn her neck. She wished she could exchange her gabled hood for one of the French ones. They looked lighter and easier to wear. Many of the French ladies wore them pushed back to expose their hair beneath. It was a vanity to be sure, but one that Ursula envied. When she was back in England she would be sure to order some for herself.

Outside the panels of her room she heard her husband calling out to her. "Are you ready? I would like for us to go together."

"Nearly. You may come in."

He stepped through, her maids curtseying quickly before returning to their hurried work.

"You look different," he said, pulling back to look at her.

A soft smile graced her even features. "I hope you approve."

"I do. The English ladies are more finely dressed than any of the French, yet there is something striking about the French."

"Could it be that they are a novelty?" Ursula teased. "What have you got there?"

He grinned, holding up the leather-bound book. "A treatise on the fall of man." Seeing her confusion he added, "I won it in a wager from Monsieur Angouleme."

"Ah. Well done. I am glad you've found some way to pass the time."

"Given what I saw today, I am glad I was a mere spectator. Do you think I'm a coward for saying so?"

Ursula shook her head. "It takes a wise man to realise when he is outmatched. I prefer you whole and healthy. These are seasoned men of war. You have time before you need to go up against them."

She could see the conflict in his eyes. He had his father's pride, and despite his words wished first and foremost to be reassured that he was the best among his peers. In the past she had been happy to reassure him of this.

Perhaps it was his sister's influence that made her speak so plainly, but just as equally she wanted to see what sort of man he was.

"And there are other ways we can impress them. Come, let us show the French we are the most learned, and beautiful court in all of Christendom," he said, holding out his hand to her.

She placed her hand in his and let him pull her to her feet, happy to know her husband was not a fool. As a general rule it was important to not rush headlong into danger and to heed the council of advisors around you. Henry may have ambitions, as any nobleman might, but he also had the wisdom to know that he lacked the experience of men like the King.

Stepping into the temporary palace, they were greeted by a chorus of beautiful music. In the rafters above, harpists plucked away at their strings. Guards were stationed throughout, not only to ensure the safety of the guests, but also to ensure lamps and brazier weren't left unattended. Fire was always a hazard, and the Val d'Or with its beautiful fabrics and tents could burn to the ground in a single moment.

They were led through the corridors to the main hall, decorated grandly with the emblems of England and France entwined to show their love and continued friendship. Given the number of people, it was a wonder that the foul smells were kept at bay. Wolsey must have arranged for a crew of diligent servants to work throughout the day.

The banquet was another marvel, but it was immediately clear there would be trouble. With so many people attending and space limited, the only strict decorum observed was at the Kings' table. Henry and Francis dined side by side; if they noticed the mayhem around them, it didn't seem to bother them.

"We should leave," Ursula said, as she was pressed into her husband by a passerby.

Henry frowned. "It's ridiculous, expecting us to fight our way through this crowd for a plate. You are right, we ought to go. It just goes to show that someone of Wolsey's calibre cannot keep control of a situation like this."

"Peace, Henry. There are far too many people in attendance. I do believe your father was restricted in how many attendants he could bring, and that was ignored. This is the most important event of our lifetime. Of course people are desperate to attend."

She didn't know whether or not he had actually listened to her, but she caught sight of Lady Elizabeth Howard making her way towards them.

"Your sister is coming to greet us," she said, nudging him.

His irritation melted away, and as she approached they embraced.

"It has been an age since I've seen you, sister."

"You as well," she said, patting his cheek affectionately. "I've already met Ursula. You have a treasure there. One you should not squander."

"I shall endeavour to keep that in mind. Have you managed to find a table for yourself?"

She shook her head. "The day has been trying and I would prefer to retire early. But I am sure this chaos will be rectified shortly. The King's marshal is taking things in hand. Did you not see the farmers and peasants lazing about the wine fountain? The whole country has turned up. It's a miracle we have enough air to breathe."

They waited until at last the guards came to clear everyone out. This was easier said than done, as many were as richly dressed as the next and it was hard to discern those impersonating noblemen from the real ones. Only the King's intervention saved the day.

At last those of rank were found seats and the banquet was allowed to resume. Sequestered near the far end of the room, Ursula's gaze flitted from one person to the next. She felt out of place, but endeavoured not to show it as Lady Elizabeth sat beside her talking animatedly. Elizabeth's husband was seated somewhere else, which suited her. Did they really not get along? Ursula's curiosity was piqued, but she didn't feel comfortable broaching the subject.

On her right, her own husband was engrossed in a debate with the King's secretary, Sir Thomas More, who'd begrudgingly come to France. Like Bishop Fisher, he was appalled by the extravagance and the waste. As More was in Wolsey's employ, she was surprised her husband was listening to him with such rapt attention.

By the time the food arrived at their table it was cold, but for all that, the meat was succulent and they ate well.

When the kings were finished eating, the remaining dishes of food were carried away to be distributed among the servants and the poor. Then the large tables were pushed against the walls to accommodate the dancing.

Both kings stood and chose a lady from the opposite court as their partner. They danced before the watching crowd and their respective queens. The kings were eager to show off their prowess and nimbly moved their partners round, at one point lifting them in the air.

When the dance ended the monarchs doffed their caps to the crowd, then turned to embrace each other again. Compliments flowed from both sides, then they retreated back to their seats and allowed the others to take centre stage.

As the evening progressed and the two queens retired, the atmosphere took a flirtatious turn and Ursula felt it was time to retreat as well.

When she placed her hand on Henry's arm, he looked disappointed to be pulled away from his conversation.

"I can escort her back to her tent if you wish, Henry," Lady Elizabeth interjected.

Ursula wished he would refuse her, but instead he was grateful for the offer. Stiffly Ursula rose, bidding him good night.

"Don't be cross with him," Lady Elizabeth said, pulling her away. "Besides, befriending Sir Thomas is a good thing."

"How so?"

"He's the King's secretary." This Ursula already knew, but she waited patiently as her sister-in-law went into further detail, expounding his many virtues and attributes. "The King values him highly. He is certainly a man you'd want to befriend. I'm sure you've seen how my father constantly tests the boundaries of propriety. The King is a jealous man and my father flaunting his wealth and royal lineage will not win him any favours."

Ursula agreed, but loyally she kept her mouth shut.

"You must ensure Henry doesn't follow in his father's footsteps," Lady Elizabeth whispered to her. Their maids and a guard were following at a distance and couldn't have overheard, but Ursula kept glancing around, worried about eavesdroppers.

"What do you mean?" she hissed.

"The King is tolerant, but even he has his limits. I fear my father tests his patience, and I worry what will happen when matters come to a head. As you must have seen, my husband and I are not... close, but I have overheard him making comments that the Duke has designs on the crown. To make matters worse, my father has made an enemy of the Cardinal." She gave a shake of her head and clutched Ursula's hand tighter.

"He's a great man but misguided in this regard. Still, I know there is little you or I can do about it. That is why I am asking you now to use whatever influence you have with Henry to have him tread a different path." She sucked in a deep breath. "Do you understand what I am trying to tell you?"

"We are in danger," Ursula deadpanned. A part of her hoped her sister-in-law would correct her, or break out into a laugh, but the gaze that met hers was unwavering in its intensity.

"This is why I am happy that Henry is eager to ingratiate himself with the King's friends. Everything we have is at the whim of the King. We all forget that from time to time."

Ursula was reminded of her own mother, and how long it had taken for her to be returned to favour. Where would they be now, had the King not felt kindly towards his York relatives? She sent up a silent prayer of thanks to God for his protection.

"Now tell me," Lady Elizabeth said, back to her exuberant self. "Did you see the cut of the French gowns?"

"They were quite different from our own," Ursula ventured.

Lady Elizabeth grinned. "Practically exposing themselves with how indecently low their necklines were. Then again, the men can't take their eyes off of them." She must have caught Ursula's expression of concern because she hurried to say, "not that Henry is looking elsewhere."

"I am not such a fool as to expect him to be loyal to me. I would prefer it, of course. What wife wouldn't? But still I hope he will not stray in front of me."

"My husband has done worse. He makes it known to everyone in our household how poorly he regards me and how highly he values his mistress."

Ursula gaped and Elizabeth nodded. "She's a mere laundress, too. Perhaps I prefer that I don't suit his tastes." She grinned, but it was a sad, melancholic smile. "Henry doesn't understand how I tolerate the insult. But if I could annul my marriage I would. Thank God for my children. They are my one joy."

"Could the Duke not—"

Elizabeth shook her head. "My father would not interfere. He'd sooner blame me for the way I am treated."

"I am sorry." Ursula had not had a father for most of her childhood, but she liked to imagine that he would have been a protector.

"It's the way of the world. We just had the rotten luck of being born women." She grinned again, some of her good humour returning. "But at least we had the good sense to be born into noble families."

The heat that had plagued them since arriving in Calais was made worse by the arrival of wind and rain.

Ursula stood at the entrance to the tent, buffeted by blasts of hot air and rain. She hugged the cloak around her to protect her fine dress.

"Should we risk it?" she asked, looking at the sodden ground.

Her husband looked uncertain, but there was determination in his gaze as he stared up at the sky. Just the previous day, the French king's tent had been destroyed by the wind and he had to flee to a nearby French castle. For now their own tent, sheltered among the others, had withstood the gale.

"It would be a shame to miss this. My mother mentioned that tomorrow you will be with her when the French king comes to dine with Queen Katherine."

Ursula nodded. "She was kind enough to ensure I would be included."

"Do you think Queen Katherine will tear off his head?" Henry whispered. Her hatred of the French was well-known, but she reserved a special dislike for their king, who had developed a reputation for his sinful ways. The Queen hated that her husband felt the need to compete with this despot.

"Of course she won't. She's far too proper to do something like that."

"Well, I daresay the French king will feel the sting of her disapproval anyhow."

Ursula shook her head.

They decided to venture out to the kings' pavilion, where the day's entertainment was being conducted. The rain had ensured most tournaments were postponed, but there was still dancing and music to be enjoyed.

As Ursula watched a troupe of mummers performing, she got the chance to speak to Katherine about Elizabeth.

"I wish I had known the two of you sooner," she said, taking a seat beside her.

Katherine smiled. "If only we could turn back time. The three of us could've run wild in the woods outside Penshurst and escaped our tutors when they tried to drill us in Latin."

Ursula chuckled, then her expression turned sombre. "Your sister misses you. She fears you are pulling away from her since your marriage. But that cannot be true, can it?"

Katherine's cheeks flushed with colour. "To be honest, I found it hard to write to her. I did not know how it would be. Especially now that my husband can see her again." She whispered this last part as though it were a shameful secret.

"You must know he has eyes for you alone."

"Yes." She went even redder. "I realise now that I am a fool."

"Only if you keep pushing her away. Speak to her. I am sure everything will be settled quite perfectly."

Katherine nodded, her eyes full of hope. "I do miss her. There is so much I wish to talk to her about." She bit her lower lip. "I have heard how awful her husband is to her. I cannot believe I ever envied her, but now I also want to help her any way I can."

Ursula squeezed her hand tightly. "You'll find a way, I am sure. Though Elizabeth doesn't strike me as someone in need of rescuing."

Katherine laughed. "No, she was always fierce. She was the only one who ever dared talk back to our father." She gave a shake of her head as she recalled the memory. "He didn't thank her for it, but I remember how Henry and I admired her bravery."

The play came to an end and Ursula clapped, along with everyone else. She felt a strong sense of pride that she was able to intervene and hoped that soon they could all have merry family parties together.

Over the following three days, the rain did not abate. The men grew bored cooped up indoors. A wrestling competition was proposed: English versus French.

Everyone was eagerly placing their bets as the gentlemen removed their jackets and took their positions to the cheers of the onlookers.

The skill of the French was obvious, but the English

had more strength, so in the end they were evenly matched and most were on the edge of their seats to see who would win.

Glancing at the King of England, it was clear to Ursula that he was displeased. His lips were pursed in a thin line and his eyes were hard as he watched an Englishman being thrown to the ground.

All at once he leapt to his feet, knocking over his goblet of wine. He turned to the French king and challenged him to a match. "Let's put this matter to rest. We shall see who is the superior wrestler."

Francis took his time dabbing the corner of his mouth with a napkin. The councillors of the two kings looked quite nervous. No one was eager for their monarchs to endanger themselves like this.

"I accept, brother." Francis stood. He was shorter than Henry and less brawny, but everyone knew wrestling was a favourite pastime of the French, and the King had been trained from a young age in the sport.

They took their places, looking undignified in their linen shirts.

Then with a nod from both, the match commenced.

King Henry was as strong as an ox and gave no ground to the French king as they grappled. After a while it was clear Henry was tired. Beads of sweat appeared on his brow and he was making mistakes.

Then in an amazing feat, the French king hooked his arm around King Henry, and with a sweep of his leg, managed to bring him down.

The French roared their approval.

Their king bowed to the crowd, flush with victory.

Ursula's eyes were on King Henry. He recovered fast enough, getting to his feet and snarling at a servant who tried to help him up.

"Again," he demanded, imperiously.

Francis shook his head. He said something Ursula could not hear, but Henry was enraged at the slight.

Rather than return to his seat and take the defeat graciously, he stormed out. His attendants hurried after him.

Wolsey apologised to the French king, who merely shrugged.

By the end of the day, the sky had cleared sufficiently that the courts could venture out to witness an archery competition. Here, at least, King Henry shone. At his invitation, the French king attempted to draw the English longbow but found he didn't have the strength for it.

"This is what won the Battle of Agincourt," King Henry boasted.

There was a glint in Francis's eyes as he turned towards his fellow monarch. "Then I am grateful for the gunpowder and crossbows that have far outstripped even this beautiful weapon on the battlefield."

King Henry, thankfully sober, had realised his misstep earlier and let the comment slide.

"We must pray that all other nations learn from our example and that one day we all come to a peaceful accord. Then weapons can become relics of a distant past."

Everyone knew the pretty words were empty. No one could envision such a utopia ever coming to be.

On the last day of the event, a chapel was erected in what had been the jousting field. Wolsey took precedence over the occasion and at the end of Mass, when the two courts exited the structure, they were greeted by an amazing sight.

Ursula gasped as, high above them, a serpentine creature, half salamander and half dragon, flew. Henry had told her the Cardinal had planned some extravagant farewell to mark the end of the meeting, but she had not envisioned such a thing.

The creature was painted on a wide strip of cloth so large that even from this distance she could make out the whites of its eyes. As it completed its journey, fireworks went off. The kings and queens once again embraced and promised undying friendship.

The business of dismantling the site of this great meeting had already begun as Ursula was helped into the saddle by her husband.

"And now for the long road back home," he sighed.

Ursula touched his brow. "I, for one, long for the comforts of home."

He brought her fingertips to his lips and placed a gentle kiss on them. "I envy your simple desires."

He misunderstood her, but she smiled down at him nonetheless. The last few days had been full of anxious moments as she watched for every sign of the King's displeasure with her husband's family. Indeed, while there was no obvious show of dislike there was a marked coldness towards them.

The King had new favourites: Nicholas Carey, Henry Norris, and the Duke of Suffolk. He heaped honours and special favours upon them, while he strove to keep the Duke of Buckingham and his party at a distance.

Even her mother, who'd once cared for King Henry when he was in the nursery and was now mistress of the precious Princess Mary, was ignored. Perhaps it was just Ursula's imagination. Maybe he resented anyone connected so strongly with his infertile wife.

Whatever it was, it kept Ursula tossing and turning at night, wondering how to interpret every word and look.

There were many occasions when she wished to speak to her husband, but the time was never right. Additionally, she didn't wish to be seen by him as the bearer of bad news, or for him to laugh and call her ridiculous.

She would bide her time and hopefully speak to him once they were alone in England.

The road back to Calais felt shorter, as their pace was no longer impeded by ceremony. Ursula hadn't properly settled into her temporary room for the evening when her chambermaid came rushing in.

"My lady," she said, bowing. "You are wanted immediately."

"What has happened?"

"Lord Henry summons you to come to his mother's rooms immediately."

"Then I shall go," Ursula said, setting down the cloak in her hand and rushing down the corridor to her mother-in-law's room. Had Henry fallen ill? Had the Duke?

Henry was pacing the room when she entered. Lady Eleanor was standing before the fire and a bedraggled messenger was standing in the corner of the room.

"Henry, what has happened?" she asked her husband, her mounting fear melting away any sense of decorum.

He stopped his pacing and she caught him blinking back tears.

"Henry?" Her gaze moved from him to her mother-in-law, who was sadly shaking her head. For a moment no one spoke or moved.

At last he came to his senses and moved towards her.

"I will tell you quickly because I cannot believe it." He paused, shutting his eyes as though he would shut out the world. "Little Harry has died suddenly, of a fever. He was dead by the time the physician came to see him. It came on fast, a-and he didn't suffer."

Ursula saw her husband, saw the fresh tears pricking his eyes, but his words were incomprehensible. "What did you say?"

"Our son is dead."

She pushed him away from her. This was a cruel joke. A lie. It could not be true. She pictured her baby in his crib, happy and healthy. When they'd left he had been chewing happily on a teething ring. She'd been so proud of his very first tooth. She choked on a sob.

"May he rest in peace. We must be comforted he is with God and his angels in heaven," Lady Eleanor said. Her composure was as cold as her words, but Ursula could see how tightly she gripped her hands before her. She wasn't as stoic as she pretended to be.

"No. He was an innocent babe. Healthy and strong. How could this have happened?" She sucked in a breath, unable to stem the flood of emotions welling up inside her. "We need to get back to England," she said to Henry. "We cannot wait."

Henry opened and shut his mouth. Clearly there was more he wished to tell her.

"Our son was buried in the family crypt. There was no way of knowing when we'd arrive. I am sorry, but all honours were given to him."

At this, Ursula wailed. She wouldn't have another chance to see her sweet child. Her first son. She wanted to go to Penshurst, throw open the doors to the nursery and find him there, sleeping in his little crib. But he wasn't there. Instead, he was gone. Buried. All alone.

Grief choked her. "I should not have come; I should've been there with him."

Henry took her by the shoulders, but she pulled away from him and ran towards her rooms. She thought she heard Lady Eleanor say, "Let her go."

She spent a day and a night crying her heart out. When her tears were spent and she was utterly exhausted, she slept. When she woke again it was only to resume crying.

On the third day, her mother came to call upon her. "Ursula, that is enough."

Ursula rolled to her side, unwilling to look at her.

"*Enough*," Lady Margaret repeated, her tone harsher and more commanding. "I didn't raise you to be a duchess only for you to waste away due to grief. Children die often. There will be others. You should be glad you are both still young and, God willing, have plenty of time to fill the nursery with other sons and daughters."

Rising on her elbows, Ursula looked defiantly at her mother. "How can you say that? You don't know what it is I feel. No child will replace the one I lost."

Her mother's stony expression made her bite her cheeks.

"You are not the only woman to suffer such a loss, nor will you be the last. Mourn as you must, but do not let yourself fall into despair like this."

Ursula felt the prick of tears in the corners of her eyes, but she fought to hold them back.

"You must be stronger than this."

They stared at each other. A silent battle of wills. Then at last Ursula sat up and allowed her mother to pull her out of bed. She was handed off to her maids who set about bathing her and changing her into a new gown. Her mother remained by her side throughout, now and again issuing commands. At no time did she allow Ursula to slip back into bed or melancholia.

Ursula was glad her mother had found her a dark, demure gown to wear. She would enter a period of mourning for her son, even if the world had never known he lived.

Her mother took the comb from a servant's fingers and eased the teeth through the tangled knots of her hair. "After you have dressed we will go to Mass, and then you will speak with my private chaplain. You must find your strength again."

"Where is Henry?" she asked, wondering why he wasn't here by her side.

Her mother paused in her ministrations. "He is preparing to leave. His father needs him to check on their lands. Duty calls him, as it will soon call you. But I have a proposition for you."

"What is it?"

"I will take you into my household, and you will travel with me to Richmond to check in on my charge. Then I shall see you safely returned home. I believe your husband thought it might be best to move to Thornbury for a while as the building projects will be taking up much of his time anyway."

"I won't return to Penshurst?"

"Not for a while. Returning so soon when the wound is still raw might be... too much for you."

Ursula blinked as she considered this. "I should like to be with you very much, lady mother." Feeling some of the weight lift from her shoulders, her mind turned to more practical matters.

"How is Henry? Have you seen him?"

"It was he who summoned me to come visit you."

"If he cared more he would've stayed himself." Ursula couldn't help but express the selfish wish.

Her mother looked at her as though she should know better. "You are lucky you have such a tolerant husband, who considers your well-being." She set down the comb and got to her feet, while the maids attached the gable hood in place.

Feeling clean and refreshed, Ursula found the strength to leave her room. The beautiful Mass, with the soothing sound of the Latin and the choir's gentle singing lifted her spirits further. When she returned to England she would order special Masses and vigils to be held for her son so he might pass from Purgatory to Heaven faster. Though, innocent as he was, she couldn't imagine he wouldn't go straight there.

The King and Queen would remain in Calais to attend

another meeting with Emperor Charles, but they dismissed half the court to return to England.

The seas were calm, so they embarked on a ship as quickly as they could. Ursula's husband had not visited her since the day they received the news about her son.

They had grown close during the Field of the Cloth of Gold, but now it felt as though a wide chasm had split them apart. How could they ever find a way to breach it? A part of her wished they had never been married. Clearly, they weren't suited to each other. Maybe they would live apart from now on.

CHAPTER 8

1520

Ursula was thrilled that her mother had allowed her to stay with her, and she slid into her household with ease, hoping that if she were helpful, Lady Margaret would change her mind and not send her back to her husband.

Richmond Palace was stunning to behold. Built on the ruins of Sheen, and set among beautiful knot gardens and orchards, King Henry had sought to create a palace that would be the envy of the world. As they rode towards it, Ursula was in awe of the red brick facade with its large windows,

Her mother smiled at her. "This is one of the King's many palaces. Warblington fades into the background compared to this. Even Penshurst cannot compete."

"Indeed, I don't think any can."

They passed beneath the main gate, where the King's coat of arms was hewn into the stone.

Once they had dismounted, her mother led her through the corridors and halls to the royal apartments, where the Princess was waiting with her nurses. Ursula felt like a peasant marvelling at the azure blue ceilings decorated with golden Tudor roses.

The four-year-old princess had stayed here while her father and mother had gone to France. Bishop Foxe and the Duke of Norfolk had been left to oversee the running of the kingdom — yet another reminder that Henry Tudor distrusted the Duke of Buckingham and wouldn't give him such a responsibility.

Ursula was once again haunted by memories of Lady Elizabeth's warning. She hadn't been able to speak to her husband, and even if he'd been here beside her she wasn't sure what she'd have said.

They curtseyed to the Princess, who leapt from her seat to run towards her governess, only to remember her manners. She stopped short of throwing her arms around Margaret. Instead she grinned, and gave her a little bob. "I am glad you have returned to me. I have prayed for your safe return. They have told me that my parents are staying behind in France for a while; I hope they shall return soon."

The Princess was precocious, and dressed in a fine gown of dusty blue. Ursula envied the beautiful slashed sleeves hemmed with seed pearls. Mary may only have been a little girl, but her manners were impeccable, and when Lady Margaret introduced Ursula, the Princess held out her hand to her to kiss.

"It's a pleasure to meet you, Your Highness," Ursula said, her smile deepening at the child's serious expression. It was rather comical to see this miniature princess act so maturely. But as her father's sole legitimate heir, she carried a lot of expectations on her small shoulders.

"You as well, Lady Ursula. Lady Margaret tells me you

are recently married. I wish to offer you my congratulations." She nodded her head primly. "Your mother has been kind to me."

Ursula shared a look with her mother, who smiled at her young charge indulgently.

They settled in at Richmond, overseeing the Princess's lessons and finding ways to keep her entertained.

Wandering around the palace was a balm to Ursula's soul. Day by day the loss of little Harry became easier to bear. She spent much of each day in the chapel, praying and lighting candles for his soul.

By the end of the second week, Ursula knew her time at Richmond was drawing to an end. She hadn't written to her husband, and he hadn't written to her. Did he think of her at all? Did he care how she was faring or wonder when she'd return to him? She suspected her mother, who spent much of the morning busy at her writing desk, was corresponding with him, or at the very least with Lady Eleanor.

This morning, Ursula and the Princess were sitting together in a large bay window, practicing their needlework. Lady Margaret was near at hand, looking over the Princess's Latin translations from the day before.

"Your mother is a very careful guardian," said the Princess.

"I am glad to hear you say so. I know she loves you and your mother dearly. And not just because you are royal." The Princess didn't look as though she believed this, so Ursula said, "Once, when I was just a bit older than you, the sweating sickness came to my home at Warblington. My nurse wrote to my mother but she dared not come because your mother was ill and needed her. She sent her love and prayers and once we were all well again she came to see us for a short time."

"You didn't mind?"

Ursula's smile was genuine as she said, "No. I am honoured my mother was such a loyal subject as to put the needs of the kingdom before that of her own family."

Princess Mary absorbed this and turned to Lady Margaret, with a serious expression. "I am glad to hear you love the realm so much. I promise to recognise your service to my family one day."

"Such solemn words for a princess," Queen Katherine said, entering the room to the surprise of them all.

They all dropped into low curtseys until she bid them rise.

Princess Mary ran to her mother, wrapping her arms around her waist. Her mother kissed her and invited Mary to sit beside her.

"The King is riding straight to Westminster to deal with some matters of state, but I took a more roundabout route to see you. I shall be happy to report to your father that you have been thriving while we were away in France."

"I have been practicing the virginals every day, and Lady Margaret says my Latin is improving."

"I am proud you've been so diligent." Queen Katherine's eyes flicked from Lady Margaret to Ursula.

Margaret stepped forward to give her report. "Her tutors say she has been applying herself and has a natural aptitude for languages and music. I brought my daughter, Lady Ursula, to spend some time with me here at Richmond and to introduce her to the Princess. She was honoured to finally have the chance to meet her." She moved forward to arrange the cushion on the Princess's seat.

The Queen turned to Ursula with a tight smile, and Ursula wondered what she meant by it. Did she remember how Ursula was a reminder that she had failed to give the King a son? She hoped not. Now she regretted her father-in-law's boast. There was no longer another generation of Buckingham heirs. A pang of fresh pain struck her and a wave of sorrow threatened to overtake her.

"What was France like? Were there tournaments? Did Father win?" the little princess interrupted.

The Queen laughed indulgently at her many questions and proceeded to recount the events to her. Ursula and her mother excused themselves so Katherine and Mary might enjoy a private moment.

"They rarely have time together like this," her mother commented. "It's always stolen moments, but that is the price you pay when you are Queen."

"I hope my presence hasn't upset her," Ursula said. "I know my father-in-law boasted about my fertility to her. It was an awkward moment."

"She knew I would be bringing you here with me. And she has faced far worse than the Duke's rudeness. I am certain there are other matters troubling her."

"I suppose I should start making plans to return home," Ursula said, as they wound their way around one of the knot gardens in the inner courtyard. She stopped to admire the marigolds.

"Yes, you are expected at Thornbury. Your husband is eager for you to return."

"Is he?" Ursula said petulantly. "Because I have not heard from him."

"Well, rest assured he has written to me. I think it was kind of him to give you time to grieve for your son. But you cannot spend your life grieving for what you have lost. Look at the Queen."

Ursula sucked in a breath. Her words hurt because they were true. She had failed her mother with this weakness, and she vowed to not let herself drown in sorrow again. Nor should she allow bitterness to fester.

"I can be ready to leave at a moment's notice," Ursula said at last.

Her mother nodded approvingly. "Good. I shall arrange everything, so take these next few days to rest." She cocked her head to the side. "You've been under my care for over three weeks. When was the last time you bled?"

Ursula did her best to recall. There had been so much to do and see, she hadn't exactly been keeping track. "Right before we departed Dover for France."

Her mother's brow arched. "Is it possible God has blessed you with another child already?" she asked softly.

Ursula's fingers splayed across her stomacher. Could it be possible? Joy flared within her at the thought. Another child could never replace the one she lost, but it would be a blessing indeed.

"I can't be sure though," she said, trying to temper her own excitement.

Her mother smiled. "You will know when you feel the child quicken in your belly. By the time you reach your husband you may have good news for him."

The journey to Thornbury was arduous. The rain had flooded the roads and the wheels of the cart kept getting trapped in the mud.

"We shall ride ahead," Ursula said at last. She was impatient to be settled in her new home. It was hard for her to keep down food, and she constantly nibbled at a loaf of bread. "Three of you will have to stay with the cart and follow behind at a slower pace."

The guards looked irritated, but they would obey her commands.

Her retinue of twenty guards in full armour and two lady's maids travelled onward. She kept a fast pace and refused to rest for long.

At last she arrived at Thornbury. The castle was not yet finished, but half of the brick building was complete. She shielded her eyes against the sun to get a better look at the oriel windows and the turrets. Innumerable chimneys jutted from the lead roof in neat orderly groups, and even before seeing inside she knew this place would rival Richmond. Certainly the gardens were extensive, if young. The knot gardens and hedges would need a few good years to grow, but she could imagine the beauty that would be here one day.

A group of riders rode out to greet her. At their head was Henry.

Tentatively she waved to him, and was happy to see him waving back.

"I have just returned from the hunt," he said, studying

her face. "When I saw you riding towards the house I thought I ought to escort you home."

She smiled. "It's good you did. I don't see the stables."

"Temporary structures have been set up around the back. We can dismount at the gate and the grooms will see to the horses."

"I am happy to know everything is in good working order here. It's certainly a beautiful location. I have never seen such a perfectly situated castle."

"Father took great care selecting the site for Thornbury. But this is nothing compared to the riches of Hampton Court. I can only imagine how much money the Cardinal has spent building and furnishing it."

"You should ask him."

Henry looked horrified by the idea, but then he laughed. "Perhaps I shall."

They led their horses towards the front of the castle and Henry helped her dismount. She felt a twinge in her belly at the movement, and a hand flew to her mouth.

"Are you well?" Henry asked, his voice full of concern. "Your mother assured me you had recovered."

"Well enough," she said, her news catching in her throat. She couldn't find the words to tell him. Not right now, with everyone watching. She had thought she'd grown stronger in the last few days, but instead found that seeing Henry only reopened old wounds.

"It was a long journey. The rain never seemed to cease and we had a tough go of it."

"I assume you abandoned your things?"

"Yes. You haven't by any chance moved the gowns from Penshurst here, have you?"

He looked uncertain. "My mother arranged everything. I am sure she considered the matter closely."

"Good," she said, looking past him to the waiting servants. "I wouldn't mind a bath, if that's possible."

"And shall I wait to have supper with you?" he asked, playing the part of the plaintiff husband. It was telling that they were on such uneasy ground that he needed to ask.

"I will eat something simple in my room. I long for a soft feather bed and a hot bath."

"In that order?"

Her expression cracked into a smile. "If you can manage it."

He offered her his arm and took her around Thornbury, proud to show off the wealth of his family and the little suggestions he had made.

"This will be your room. Mine is the adjoining one. They aren't as large as at Penshurst but this will be temporary while they finish the other wing of the house. They are comfortable enough." He was tripping over his words, desperate to make sure she was pleased. It was also a way to fill the silence and give her no room to dredge up the past.

"Henry, I've slept in a tent, spent weeks on the road and on a ship. A warm room with a roof overhead is plenty for me."

He snorted. "I'll remember that."

"Will you come see me tonight?" Her voice was soft but she didn't plead with him. "Once I've got some of this dirt off then I will feel like a person again."

He glanced away. She'd never known him to be cowardly, but it appeared he was nervous to be alone with her. They would have to try to repair their relationship. Especially if they were to have another child.

"I am happy to be here, Henry," she said. *With you,* was implied but left unsaid.

He took her hand in his and gave it a gentle squeeze. "I am glad you're back."

Judging by the glowing embers left in the grate, it had grown late. Ursula sipped on the mulled wine, swirling it around the cup.

At last she heard the rap of a knuckle on her door and called out, "Come in."

Henry stepped through, dressed for bed, a long robe tied tightly up to his neck.

"How are you settling in?" he asked, standing near the door, looking half ready to run.

"Even in this unfinished state, Thornbury is beautiful."

He nodded. "My father spared no expense." He scratched the back of his neck, looking anywhere but at her.

"Sit by me and tell me what is on your mind," she urged him, hoping she sounded conciliatory. He took a seat, but his posture was rigid.

"Henry," she murmured. "There's much to say. For my part I am sorry for how I stormed out and refused to see you. I still think of our little son every day and I wish... things had been different but I'm coming to accept what I cannot change. I hope we can move past this and be... close again."

He reached for her hand, his expression softening, and

she thought she caught the glint of tears in his eyes before he turned his face away and sniffed.

"I should've been more insistent, but it felt like it was for the best that you had time to deal with the loss—"

She interrupted, "Our loss."

"Ours," he agreed. There was a long pause as they withdrew from each other. "I grieve too. He was my son and would've one day been Duke after me. At the same time — I acknowledge I didn't see him as often as I should have. I thought there'd be time to watch him grow. To teach him to hold a sword—"

"S-stop." Ursula choked on a sob. "I'm sorry. I can't, it's too much." She put a hand to her chest. "I wish it would stop feeling like this."

Henry knelt before her, cupping her face in his hands. They didn't speak, just stared into each other's eyes. Understanding passed between them as they shed tears.

"Regret is a bitter pill to swallow. But grief is a poison." He kissed her cheek.

"Then I should give you some joyous news to wash the misery away. I believe I am with child. It is early days and I can't be sure, but I've been sick in the mornings."

Henry looked stunned. His breath was shaky as he said, "That would — that would be the happiest news you could've brought me."

She nodded, turning away from him because now it was time she shared with him what his sister had said.

He listened patiently, but his expression was incredulous. "My father — he just wants his due."

"But if he pushes the King too far, he shall bring us down."

"I heard he keeps going against the King's express wishes. I didn't hear all the details but he cannot keep butting heads with him. Not unless he is certain of victory." Henry took a turn about the room, his mind whirling at her news. "He disapproves of who the King is favouring. You must see it yourself. He elevated Charles Brandon to the status of a duke. Allowed the cad to marry his sister. The King's sister! She could've made another grand royal marriage. But it is useless to list everything."

"You are right. It is useless because the point is moot. The King will do as he wishes. We are fools for setting ourselves up against him. It's been years since your father has had any position at court because he is not trusted, and yet, rather than learning to toe the line, he has further exacerbated matters. You must see how dangerous this is."

Perhaps she'd gone too far, but Henry looked resigned. Deep down he must know she was right.

"Father petitioned the King to raise an armed force to patrol the Welsh borders."

Ursula was stunned by this. Such a request at a time like this appeared suspicious to say the least.

"The year of our marriage, the King demanded my father take stronger action to bring order to the Welsh Marches. Now he's determined to do just that."

"And nothing else?"

"As far as I know," Henry said.

"Pardon me for saying it, but this looks — bad. Why didn't he act sooner?"

Henry rounded on her. "Are we to be his judges, then?"

"Better us than anyone else."

"I know. I know." He ran his hands through his hair. It

was clear his anger wasn't directed at her; he was exasperated at the situation.

"I'm sure there's time. Speak to your father. See if he will be more circumspect about how he acts and what he says. This could all be nothing but, it's better to be cautious."

"I will," Henry said, but he looked pale and uncertain. His father was a domineering man who didn't like to be challenged. "Now let us put this aside and speak of happier things. When do you think the baby will be due?"

"January."

With her great round belly, Ursula felt more like a stuffed cushion than a beautiful lady of the manor.

They were celebrating the Christmas season at Thornbury. The Duke had business in Wales, and Thornbury was well placed. It was quickly becoming apparent that he wished for Thornbury to eventually become his primary residence, and he spared no expense in furnishing it.

The liveable areas of the house may have been smaller than at Penshurst, but they were comfortable and lavish. The plastered walls insulated each room while the painted frescos added colour and beauty. In the library and dining hall, intricately carved wood panelling lined the walls and guests walked on beautiful ceramic tiles painted with the family crest. It was luxurious indeed.

The Duke and Henry had ridden out through the Welsh Marches, finally addressing the concerns of the locals. Order was restored as criminals were caught and tried, inheritances properly dispersed and legal disputes settled. The whole venture had proved to be successful.

Henry returned energised and confident in his own abilities. He confessed that his father had been eager to let loose his armed guard on the people who so blatantly disrespected him, wishing to instil fear and obedience. Henry had prevailed upon him to set up a makeshift court and hear all their concerns.

The Duke took to riding out to hunt in the region, leaving his son to oversee everything.

"I can manage a sword just fine," said Henry, "but my true skill lies in debates."

Ursula smiled indulgently, smoothing a hand over her belly as the child inside gave a mighty kick. "And yet this troubles you?"

"It is hardly a noble pursuit. I fear I disappointed my father."

"He has said as much?"

"No, but I can see it in his eyes." Henry looked away.

"Well, I believe, as Erasmus wrote in one of his essays, that a noble prince needs to excel at more than just combat. He must be a paragon of virtue, promoting peace and upholding the law of the land."

He strode over and placed his hand on her belly, grinning when he felt the child stirring beneath.

"I don't know how I am to bear it for two more months, Henry," Ursula groaned. "I truly don't."

"At least you have Elizabeth for company."

"Truly that was a surprise." She smiled up at him. "However did you convince her to come?"

"She didn't take much convincing. Spending the Christmas season alone at Kenilworth didn't appeal to her."

"I hope she and the Earl can come to an understanding," Ursula said. "Perhaps you can play the role of mediator."

"I am wise enough to know that even some things are beyond me. Now, shall I call your ladies to help prepare you for bed?"

"Yes, please. Tomorrow we shall rise early to celebrate Saint Stephen's day Mass and then hand out alms. I believe your mother has seen to everything. We need only attend."

"You sound almost bitter."

Ursula met his gaze and shrugged. "Sometimes I think I have nothing to do here but be a broodmare and toil over needlework, while contributing little to the household."

"Nonsense." He placed a tender kiss on her brow. "Now I must bid you goodnight."

Irritably, she scowled. "Don't pretend you are off to bed yourself. I know you and your friends are planning on drinking the night away and gambling."

He had the decency to look sheepish.

"Just think of me from time to time. I am tucked away in this tower, exhausted by the mere thought of walking down the stairs. Pity me."

"No one could," he said. With a flourish he bowed and was gone.

She watched the door and then struggled to her feet to go look out the oriel window. The outer courtyard was covered with a thin dusting of snow. The moon was full and cast long shadows over the landscape. She thought she saw a shadow running along the hedgerow, but was distracted when the door to her chamber opened and Lady Elizabeth stepped through.

"Good evening, I thought I'd keep you company," she said, coming to stand beside her. "Did you see something?"

"I thought I did but I must be imagining it."

"It's probably some servant sneaking out for a late night tryst." Lady Elizabeth pulled her away from the window. "Come sit in your bed and I will entertain you with gossip from the court."

"I feel like you are my nursemaid."

"Then you should be glad that I am so kind and gentle," she said, pulling back the covers and furs on the feather bed. The intricately carved bed frame was decorated with lions, and on the headboard above her was the Buckingham crest.

Ursula would've selected pleasanter designs. Her mother's bed had been decorated with carvings of beautiful gardens. But alas, every night and morning the crest greeted her with a reminder of her duty to provide children for the Duke's dynasty.

She removed her heavy robe, leaving only a simple linen night shift, before climbing into bed. "So — tell me everything."

Lady Elizabeth had been at court until two weeks ago. She drew up a stool to the bedside and lit the candle on the table nearby. "The King is in love."

Ursula's eyes widened. "With who?"

"No one knows for certain," she said with a haughty grin.

"But you do," Ursula guessed.

Elizabeth nodded, her pleasure tempered. "Truth be told, it brings me no joy to know that once again another lady caught the King's attention. Queen Katherine is a good woman and deserves his love and respect."

"Yes. My mother must be beside herself. Who is it?"

"Mary Carey. Sir Thomas Boleyn's daughter."

Ursula was stunned. "But she's a lady of the bedchamber! My mother said she was loyal to the Queen."

Elizabeth rolled her eyes. "Bessie Blount was, as well. Perhaps the King finds it convenient to look for mistresses among the ladies of his wife's rooms."

"That is terrible. But I suppose I shouldn't be surprised that Mary would be willing to risk her reputation like this. Her husband is a courtier, friends with the King. What must he be thinking?"

"It's being kept quiet. Nothing much has happened, as far as I'm aware, besides little gifts and poems. I only know because of my husband. He's always sniffing around for an opportunity to rise in the King's favour."

"Bessie Blount's family saw little reward." Ursula wrinkled her nose at the distasteful thought of lowering herself to adultery for a few scraps of land and coin.

"She's done well enough for herself. If her son is the King's only male child — well, who knows."

Ursula shook her head. "There's time. The Queen could still have a son."

"The Queen has gone on pilgrimage to Walsingham to pray for that very thing."

"Poor Lady."

"Now, not all my news is sad. I have sketched a few of the new fashions I have seen being worn at court." Lady Elizabeth handed her sheaths of paper on which were drawings of round-necked gowns braided with silk cords. "And since we returned from France, French hoods have been all the rage."

"Beautiful. I shall have to set the seamstress to work. Once this baby is out, I shall reward myself with more gowns."

Elizabeth chuckled. "Careful, or you will become the envy of all English women. I wouldn't be surprised if you have more dresses than the Queen herself."

"They make me happy," Ursula sniffed. "But I know greed is a sin."

"Yet you are stubbornly set in your ways?"

Ursula handed the papers back to her friend. "For now."

The following day, dressed in sombre black and tawny browns, the family processed to the church to hear Mass. At the end, the box of alms was brought forth and everyone in the family, including the Duke himself, distributed them among the poor waiting outside.

Choruses of 'God bless' were heard throughout the churchyard.

The Duke had also paid for the monastery to host a great banquet for all who would attend.

Back inside Thornbury's walls, they distributed more coins and other small gifts to their servants. For entertainment, the family was determined to ride out on the snowy ground. The snow was not deep and it wouldn't be dangerous to do so.

In honour of Saint Stephen, the patron saint of horses, they went to decorate the horses in the stable with ribbons and bells. Ursula was too far advanced in her pregnancy to consider riding out herself, but she ensured her beautiful mare would be decked out in pretty trimmings. Henry had promised he would exercise her himself.

"Belle is displeased with me," Ursula said, patting her horse's neck. Her coat was soft as silk.

Elizabeth came over and offered the horse some oats. "She's as spoiled as her owner. She doesn't handle disappointment well."

Ursula laughed but nudged her sister-in-law with her elbow. "You make me sound like a spoiled brat." She used the comb to brush out Belle's mane and began to braid it.

"You have everything you could possibly want," Elizabeth pointed out.

Ursula's hand stilled. That wasn't exactly true. Memories of Little Harry swam to the forefront of her mind and a wave of grief passed over her.

"I am sorry. I was only teasing," Elizabeth said, softly.

"You are right. I am luckier than most. Henry dotes on me now. I could have my room gilded with gold if I wished and he wouldn't deny me." Ursula tied the end of the braid and attached a little silver bell.

From the upper gallery she watched as the party of close family and friends rode out to the deer park. They kicked up the snow as they galloped, the sound of tinkling bells filling the air.

Her child moved about in her belly and she rubbed at the spot, hoping to soothe him.

In a low tone she began to sing an old carol:
"Lullay my liking,
My dear Son, my Sweeting,
Lullay my dear Heart,
Mine own dear Darling."

After the day of charity and almsgiving came the day of frivolity. The third day of Christmas was given over to drink and games in honour of Saint John the Evangelist, who survived a poisoning of wine. As was tradition in those households that could afford it, ale and other beverages were set aside in favour of rich red wines.

The Duke had imported varieties from as far as Gascony. Having not been invited to court for the Christmas season, he was determined to outshine the King here at Thornbury. Many of his vassals and tenants were in attendance. Over the last few days, hundreds of people had eaten and celebrated with them.

Ursula's nausea had never abated and she sipped at a cup of hot spiced wine as casket after casket of wine was opened and shared with the guests and household.

Beside her at the high table, Henry's cheeks were pink with drink and she laughed as he clambered to his feet to give a toast.

"To Ki-ing. Country. And Duke."

"Amen," she said with a grin. Ursula might not be drunk but she could amuse herself with the antics of others.

The Duke was far drunker than his son. He staggered as he moved about the hall, patting his friends on the back with far too much force. Some choked on the food they were eating, which only made him laugh.

"Rightfully all three titles belong to me," called the Duke. "Am I not descended from Edward III? Who else besides me has the right to the throne?" He hiccupped and pushed away a server who came forward to take his cup from him. He raised it, and the wine sloshed around, spilling and staining the sleeve of his coat blood red. "May the Queen remain as fruitful as she is now."

It was a cruel jest.

Some laughed, but many more looked uncomfortable, unsure how to react to such treasonous talk.

Ursula, sober and with her wits about her, glanced around the room. Her mother-in-law's lips were pinched in a tight line of disapproval, but she didn't try to stop her husband. Some were openly glaring in the Duke's direction. She hoped the situation could be rectified.

The Duke continued in his tirade. "I hope in the future the King will think of me kindly and acknowledge I belong at his side. No more should the likes of Wolsey and Brandon have run of the realm. They are not worthy enough to wipe my boots."

Ursula placed a hand on her husband's sleeve. Their eyes met, and she saw her own worry mirrored there.

As the Duke took another cup of wine, Henry approached him and pulled him away from the dining hall.

Since she could not shut her ears to the sounds of shouting that followed, Ursula closed her eyes. Her husband returned, his expression grim. His mother rose to her feet and slid out of the room. Ursula hoped she had gone to speak to him. Perhaps she would have better luck.

Then, in order to not extend the awkward moment any longer, Ursula called out to the musicians, "Play on."

On New Year's Day, Ursula awoke to find her room filled with sprigs of rosemary and garlands of holly. Her walls were hung with cloth of every colour.

"What is this, Henry?" she said with a smile.

"My sister has been speaking to me about your plans for new gowns once you have been churched," Henry said, placing a hand on her belly. His soft smile melted away her worries. "I was determined to raid the merchants' carts of every bolt of cloth I could find."

"I don't see any homespun wool," she teased.

He grinned. "I shall amend my previous statement to specify only the best cloth was chosen to grace your chambers. If you approve of them I shall have them all tucked away from a later time."

"I do approve of them." Ursula laughed. "I consider myself very spoiled."

"This is not everything, but to see the rest you must get dressed and leave your bedchamber."

"What more could you have done?" she asked, her eyes widening. A fortune was already hanging on her walls.

"Ah, I shall not tell," he said. "I will await you outside."

Her maids came forward, smiling, and helped her dress as quickly as possible. The only gowns that still fit her had to be left with the stomacher unlaced. She allowed them to put on a beautiful English-style gown, finding its shapelessness more accommodating for her growing belly. It was made of a navy blue damask decorated with beautiful floral embroidery. Her hair was left tumbling down her back before they put on a French hood, a gift from her sister-in-law. It was black satin with seed pearls. She exchanged the veil for a blue one to match the gown.

Finally ready, she emerged. Her husband was waiting beside a table on which was something wrapped in black velvet.

"Close your eyes," he said before she got a good look at it.

Doing as he bid, she felt his hand wrap around her elbow and lead her forward. After he had placed her just so, he urged her to look.

She was stunned by the wealth before her. He'd uncovered a necklace of gold and rubies, with matching earrings and bracelet.

"Oh, Henry," she sighed, letting her fingers glide over the finery. "This is too much."

"You are my lady and you deserve nothing less."

"I have something for you as well." She motioned for her maid, who was holding a large wooden box, to come forward. Removing the carved lid, Ursula revealed a beautiful chain, its links interspersed with black jet stones the size of her palm.

"The King of France had such a chain, and I thought it would suit you."

"Thank you," he said, kissing her cheek. "I doubt there's another lord and lady in the kingdom who will be more fashionably dressed than us."

Normally she would've scolded him for his boasting, but she couldn't help but agree.

"There's one other thing I would wish you to see," he said, "though you won't be able to use it yet."

"Now you wish to shame me, for I have nothing else for you."

"It's not a competition." He smirked. "But if it was, I

would've won."

She swatted at his arm.

Arm in arm, they walked down the long corridors to the gallery, and he guided her to the windows overlooking the inner courtyard. Among the knot gardens she saw her mare, Belle, a groom holding on to her reins. Against the snow, her black coat shone. She was tacked up with a beautiful harness of crimson velvet, fringed with cloth of gold.

"I know how you love to ride. Do you like it?" Henry asked.

She was incredulous. "Of course I do."

"Good. My parents have something else for us."

He took her to the solar, where her mother-in-law and sister waited. As she entered, they held out a beautiful blue christening gown lined with ermine. "For all your children to wear."

Tears welled in Ursula's eyes. "It's — I'm speechless. Thank you," she said, curtseying to them, as was customary.

"The children you bear will carry on the family name. There is nothing to be grateful for," her mother-in-law said coolly, but Ursula could see she was pleased by the compliment.

"I helped with the lacing," Elizabeth said, pointing out the soft frills around the collar. "I am glad you like it, for I have gone half-blind in the making of it."

Her mother shot her a look of disapproval but Ursula quickly interjected.

"My children shall be raised to appreciate what a caring aunt they have. And when you are old and far too frail, I shall send you my daughters to do all your needlework."

Elizabeth laughed. "I shall hold you to that."

More gifts were exchanged and then the family heard Mass. The New Year's feast was just as grand as Christmas Day. The Duke had hired a troupe of actors to perform a beautiful tableau of King Arthur in battle against the Black Knight. Ursula tried not to see it as an allegory, but the Duke was dressed as finely as any King, and the Black Knight had a red rose on his helmet. Surely it was a coincidence — her father-in-law would not dare portray himself as the rightful King of England battling Henry Tudor. Surely not.

Thanks to the beautiful performance and the choir singing, Ursula was able to forget her misgivings and she cheered with the rest of the family as the performers bowed. She rewarded the troupe with a small purse.

Later there was dancing, and she was forced to enjoy the music from the sidelines as her husband danced around the room, his attention drifting from one lady to the next. His gaze often lingered, and was filled with a heat that told her it was far from innocent. Had it not been for her belly, she would have joined the throng and kept his attention on herself.

He had not visited her bed since she had told him she was with child. Ursula didn't expect him to remain faithful, but she didn't enjoy being reminded that although he could be thoughtful, Henry was not loyal to her, as he ought to be. She tried to swallow down the bitter feeling welling up inside her, knowing it might harm the child she carried. Besides, it was beneath her to be concerned about the infidelity of men. What mattered was that after the dancing, he returned to her side.

The following day her sister-in-law left them, as the roads were good and the weather looked clear.

"Write to me often," Elizabeth said, as they embraced. "Keep me abreast of how you do. I shall pray for you."

"Thank you," Ursula said. "I am eager for this child to be born." Her gaze shifted to Henry nearby. His attention kept drifting from his friends to the pretty servant girl that had eyed him as she walked by.

"Men." Elizabeth scowled. "Don't let it bother you. He cares for you and values you. In recent years, he has become more responsible. It's all owing to your influence."

"Thank you for saying so, but I would prefer our household not to be littered with his bastards."

Her sister-in-law laughed. "What wife doesn't wish that?"

With her departure, Ursula lost a companion for the long winter days, when her belly kept her confined to her rooms. Henry visited her every morning but he was distracted, and once she entered confinement he settled on sending her small gifts and notes. What she wanted was to see him. These little tokens meant nothing.

CHAPTER 10

1521

"Let me see them!"

She heard Henry's voice calling from beyond the door. The midwife let out an annoyed groan as she hurried along.

Ursula watched as they bathed her son and he gave a loud scream.

Henry's voice came again.

"Let him see the baby," she urged. "He won't stop until he does."

The midwife gave a curt nod and handed the baby to Lady Eleanor, who was waiting nearby. "Another son, you are blessed," her mother-in-law said.

"Bring him right back," said Ursula.

"Of course." Lady Eleanor's voice was soothing.

The chambermaids rushed about removing the soiled sheets, and cut away the stained shift she'd worn during the labour. It had been an easier birth than the last. When her waters broke there had been barely enough time to call the midwife and boil the water before the baby's head emerged.

123

She sent up another prayer of thanks that her son was born strong and healthy. This time he would live. She wouldn't leave his side.

Lady Eleanor brought back the baby, who was scrunching up his face in displeasure.

"He's hungry," Ursula said. "Where's the wet nurse?"

"Right here, my lady." A woman stepped forward.

Lady Eleanor passed the baby to her and she sat down to feed the child.

Ursula watched, but her eyes shifted to Lady Eleanor who was looking pensively at her new grandson. "What is wrong?"

She shook her head. "Henry has picked a name for him."

Ursula's lips pursed. It was a father's right to name the child, but she had a feeling she wouldn't like it.

"He wants him to be called Henry, after the King, of course."

The two women shared a knowing look. He was trying to replace their lost son with this one. But he was wrong, this wouldn't erase their memories of their first son.

"As he wishes," Ursula said, laying back on the pillow. Her first instinct had been to fight, but she couldn't bring herself to.

"May he come in to see you?" Lady Eleanor looked about the room. The smell of blood still hung in the air, but the evidence of the birth had been cleared away.

"Yes."

"Very well," she said, giving her hand a squeeze. The gesture, so simple and comforting, made Ursula remember her mother's tender care after the death of her first child, and she found she missed her fiercely.

Henry appeared at her side moments later, blinking against the darkness as he looked at her.

"Thank God you are well," he said. "I — our son is beautiful. He looks strong," he ventured.

"He does."

"That is good."

She could see the unvoiced question in his eyes: *Will he live longer than the last?* Ursula was reminded he had not deigned to pay attention to their first child. Nor had he rushed into the birthing chamber, defying all convention as he had done now.

"I brought you something," he said, and unfurled a small package in front of her, revealing a leather-bound book encrusted with gems. "It's a book of hours. They say it was blessed by the Archbishop of Canterbury. I thought you might like it. And father has ordered a new crib for Henry," he said, testing the name.

She caught his frown, but then saw him brush aside the unease.

"Thank you." She placed a weary hand on it, finding she didn't have the energy to flip through the pages.

"Rest and recover your strength. I shall see you as soon as you are churched." He leaned over her and kissed her brow.

She watched him go, wondering if she would've preferred him to stay away.

Over the next few weeks, she recovered her strength and was soon up and about. Congratulations poured in, along with gifts for her little son, but she barely glanced at the plates of gold, the jewels and the bolts of cloth. Perhaps it was her already immense wealth that made the gifts seem insignificant. All she wanted was for her son to continue to thrive, and no one could promise her that.

If she had been able to choose Henry's godparents, she would've chosen Lady Elizabeth, for she had been a good friend to her. But the Duke picked the Earl of Westmorland. Her little son was whisked from her rooms one morning and put in the beautiful blue velvet she'd received as a gift at New Year. He was returned a few hours later with assurances he'd done well.

When at last she was churched, and emerged from the darkened chamber, she was happy to find the house quiet. In fact, it was too empty. The Duke of Buckingham had gone to visit the Carthusian monks at Sheen, while her husband had ridden out to deal with some dispute over an inheritance of farmland. He should've returned by now but had been delayed by bad weather.

Her mother-in-law was sitting in the solar in the bright early morning sun, stitching away at a screen. It was a beautiful forest scene. A deer was running through the trees with a pack of hounds chasing after it. The details were extraordinary, as was the way she'd used gold thread to add movement and life to the piece.

It was then Ursula noted the silence. She paused to listen, realising the constant noise of construction at Thornbury was gone.

Curious, she asked, "Is there some delay? Henry wrote to me that the wood panelling in the new wing would be installed over the winter."

"The Duke has had some disagreements with the

surveyor about the mounting costs. He's been released from service. So while Sir Robert hires someone new to oversee the project, we shall enjoy some peace and quiet."

"And where is Sir Robert? I wish to see him about the household expenses. I need an increase on my quarterly allowance."

"Whatever for?" Lady Eleanor was tightfisted when it came to money that wasn't to be spent on herself, or the house.

"My expenses are mounting and I wish to fund a hospital in the monastery in Henry's honour."

"A charitable endeavour. When Sir Robert is back from London we shall speak with him."

"London?" Ursula asked, surprised.

"He's visiting family. My husband gave him permission. I believe his father is ill."

"Ah, I am sorry to hear it."

Ursula didn't know why the news made her uneasy. Hadn't he mentioned his family was from Devon? As she took a seat and began stitching her son some linen shirts, she shook the worries from her mind.

Her husband returned to her brimming with energy and optimism. "It feels like a fresh start," he said, lifting her into the air and spinning her round. "You are looking more beautiful than ever, our son is healthy, and my father is entrusting me with more responsibilities."

She laughed. "Just in time for spring too. May all your hopes blossom."

"I have other news for you. Your brother Arthur is getting married. Would you like to attend the wedding?"

"Of course I would. Do you know who my mother settled on? She only alluded to the match she was thinking of."

"Do you know Lady Jane? I believe she is a young widow, but—"

"— an heiress. Yes, my mother wouldn't match him with anyone who wouldn't bring in a proper dowry."

"Why do you sound cross? Do you disagree with your mother? Marriages must be made for the benefit of both families, in terms of strengthening ties and financial benefit."

"I know all that. But it's certainly not romantic."

He tapped her nose. "Have you been reading chivalric tales, my dear?"

She scrunched up her nose and moved away from him. "No. Nothing like that. I suppose we can't all live in a fairy story. But I am happy for him and I hope they will be well suited. My eldest brother made a fabulous match. They are quite happy together; they have a daughter already."

"Since you are so busy thinking of your brother's happiness, why not turn your attention to our son's future? We must dig up an heiress for him to marry one day."

She scoffed. "It's far too soon for that."

Henry looked put out, as though she doubted their son would live long enough to get married.

"Henry," she cooed. "At this very moment, your son is happiest being held by the poor, tired nursemaid. He cannot sleep unless he's being constantly rocked. If we are so concerned about his happiness we can think about hiring him another maid to care for him."

Her husband grinned. "Whatever the little duke wants, he shall have."

"As long as our purse can manage it." She smiled sheepishly. "I do believe we've overspent this quarter. I hope Robert Gilbert will be well disposed to give us a larger stipend."

"I'll speak to my father."

Henry's solution would do for now. Ursula didn't want to think about what would happen in the future, when he was duke. His chancellor could never dictate to him how he should spend their money, but it was within their best interest to curtail expenses and grow the family fortune rather than spend it.

Ursula watched as they bathed her little son. He was two months old now and growing plumper by the day. There had been an outbreak of disease in the village but for now it had not entered the castle. She had forbidden any of her precious son's servants to venture out beyond the castle gates lest they bring back some contagion.

The atmosphere at Thornbury was tense. The Duke had arrived back from his duties in Wales in a dark mood. Shortly thereafter, he left to tour his estates and visit his relatives. Work on the castle had ceased, and Ursula wondered if funds were tight.

"Has something happened to make your father cross?"

"He has not told me," Henry said. "But he has given us

permission to go to Warblington to attend your brother Arthur's wedding. Do you still wish to go?"

"I do." She bit her lower lip. "If you are sure it won't upset him or your mother."

"No. Besides, they are our family too." He grinned. "In the future we may need them."

"What do you mean by that?"

"Nothing," he said quickly, and it made her suspicious.

"Henry, has something happened? You can tell me," she said, placing a hand on the embroidered sleeve of his jacket.

"Some of our servants have been questioned by Wolsey's men and brought to London. It's nothing."

Her breath caught in her throat. "What do you mean, nothing?"

"We've done nothing wrong, and thus have no reason to fear him questioning our men. Wolsey is overstepping the mark. He has no business looking into our affairs, but there's nothing for him to find so let him look."

"But Henry, the King must have given him permission to act."

"And they will find nothing. He means to unsettle us and try to scare us, but he will find we are made of sterner stuff," he said confidently. But rather than wait to hear her response, he pushed past her and left her alone. He didn't wait to hear her concerns that the Cardinal could simply order the men tortured until they confessed to some terrible crime. Innocence didn't matter if Wolsey had decided to move against the Duke. And most worryingly of all, Henry was wrong. The Duke had given the King plenty of reason to doubt him.

In his nursery, Harry cried and she took him from the

nurse to rock him in her arms. She held him tightly, her eyes on the door as if, any moment now, the King's men might rush in and take him away from her.

Arthur married Jane in a simple ceremony in the family chapel at Warblington. Ursula stood proudly beside her mother as the couple exchanged their vows.

Afterwards, in the great hall, Arthur led Jane to meet her. "Jane, this is my sister, Lady Ursula."

"It's a pleasure to meet you," Jane said, curtseying low. Her eyes took in Ursula's rich dress but she quickly disguised her envy behind a smile.

"I've travelled a long way to see you," Ursula said, kissing her cheeks. "You look beautiful. I wish you every joy in your marriage and I hope you will like the gifts I have brought you. Bolts of Flemish cloth and Italian silk."

Jane flushed pink, thrilled at the prospect.

"You are too generous, Lady Ursula," she said, eyes downcast.

"It's no less than you deserve." She turned her attention to Arthur. "Make sure to write to me if my brother doesn't treat you as he ought to."

He laughed. "I shall give her no cause to complain."

"Good."

Casting a glance around the room she wondered where Henry had gone.

"I believe he's slunk off with Geoffrey to play cards," Arthur said, guessing who she was looking for.

His attention to her ebbed and flowed like the tide. She

shouldn't expect more from him, and yet, she did. Trying her best not to show how much it bothered her, she went to find her mother. Lady Margaret Pole may have been forty-eight, but she looked strong as an ox. It was hard to imagine her mother as elderly, but she was quickly approaching the age when she would think of retiring and allowing her heir greater responsibility. Ursula still saw her as a rock who could weather any storm, and now she needed her advice.

"Lady Mother, may I speak to you?"

Her mother eyed her. "About what?"

"I suspect you know the King is displeased with the Duke."

"That is old news. I am sure the Duke will come to his senses and apologise to the King. He may be forced to continue his exile for a while, but there is nothing to concern yourself about."

"Some of our servants have disappeared." Ursula leaned close to whisper in her mother's ear. "I fear we are being watched."

Her mother pulled away but her features remained devoid of emotion. "When?"

"A few weeks ago. Whether they were arrested or went willingly is unclear. Do you know something?"

Her mother shook her head. "I have been with the Princess, and then the Queen gave me leave to return home to prepare for this wedding. There has always been friction between the King and the Duke of Buckingham. But what could he be accused of?"

"Nothing," Ursula said stoically, defending her father-in-law. "I fear the Cardinal is behind this."

"I will see what I can discover and I will write to you."

"Would it be safe to do so?"

Her mother's lips curled into a half-smile at her naivete. "I shall see that a message is sent to you in secret. We don't have time to decide upon a secret code but I will send you the note by your brother Geoffrey so that you know it's from me."

Ursula was reminded that her mother had survived many upheavals and dangers to get to where she was today. Perhaps she was not as passive in them as she pretended to be. "Thank you, lady mother."

Her mother placed a hand on Ursula's cheek and lifted her face up to look at her. Studying her for a moment, she said, "You are tired, I can see it in your face. Ursula, it is important to remember you are not powerless. But at the same time you must accept you cannot be everywhere all at once. The games of politics are fraught with danger. In time your husband will become one of the premiere men of the land. You must cast aside your anxieties."

It was easier said than done. Her mind was always plagued with doubt and it was hard to see the light past the shadow.

The feast in Arthur's honour carried on into the night and she played the part of the carefree lady perfectly. Her husband returned, having drunk far too much wine, and they twirled together on the dancefloor before slipping away to their chambers.

She didn't speak to Henry about her conversation with her mother. He was determined to pretend nothing was happening and so she followed suit.

They spent the next few weeks wrapped up in frivolous pursuits. Ursula attended to their son, then in the afternoons rode out hunting and hawking with her husband. She didn't question why the Duke hadn't dismissed his armed retinue, keeping them instead at Thornbury. She looked away from the increasing number of carts arriving at the castle filled with dried provisions and treasure from the Duke's other homes. If she stopped to think about it for too long, she might conclude he was preparing for a battle. Perhaps it would be better for her to gamble and drink herself silly, like her husband did. Then she could numb the growing sense of unease.

In April, a messenger arrived from Windsor with an official summons for the Duke. Ursula was in the great hall when her father-in-law received him. He heard the news with good cheer but Ursula saw the uncertainty in his eyes before he steadied himself.

Her husband turned to his father and asked, "Will you go?"

"Of course," the Duke said, with an eye to the King's messenger. "I welcome the chance to obey the King."

"And I shall accompany you, Your Grace," the messenger said with a bow of his head.

The Duke's smile wavered but he gave a curt nod. "As you please." He motioned for his steward to step forward. "Ensure everything is packed and ready to go at first light tomorrow." For a moment his gaze flicked to the messenger, who didn't contradict this or suggest he leave sooner.

All this was a mere show. Everyone knew the Duke had no choice but to comply with the King's summons. There was to be a reckoning, and Ursula, waiting behind a pillar, clutched at her pearl necklace, the beads digging into her palm.

The Duke strode out of the hall to his private apartments, Henry following on his heels. As Henry passed her, his eyes caught hers and she saw the fear in them.

Henry was worried for his father and wished to ride to London with him, but as the family gathered to discuss the situation, the Duke overruled him.

"You will remain here and look after my affairs with your wife and son. I will hear no more on the subject."

Like a chastened child, Henry hung his head, but he knew better than to argue. Besides, his father was right, it was better to remain behind. If the Cardinal was to swoop in with some foul trick, at least he wouldn't capture both father and son together.

Ursula, holding her son, was among those who bid the Duke farewell as he rode out with a small guard and his steward. He said farewell to them all with a booming, confident voice. Then he kissed his wife and knelt for her blessing. He paused a moment in front of Ursula to study his grandson's face, and smiled as the child gurgled.

Then he mounted his horse and rode out.

Three days later they were brought news of his arrest.

CHAPTER 11

As news of the Duke's arrest spread, many servants fled. They had seen which way the wind was blowing and weren't going to risk being brought down with the family if they remained.

The Duchess locked herself in her rooms, allowing only her confessor to see her.

Henry was beside himself with worry for his father, and it was useless to speak to him. Overcome by worry, he fell into a depression that kept him confined to his bed, or at his desk writing letters he never sent.

Ursula was left to manage the household. She ensured that her son was seen to and had every comfort.

As she wandered down the silent halls, she wondered what the Duke's arrest would mean for the family. Of all the endless possibilities, none were good. Even if the King released the Duke tomorrow and the two men made peace, the Duke would never be the same again. Everyone would know he wasn't untouchable. His enemies would swarm and find a way to tear him down.

A week later a bedraggled Geoffrey rode into the courtyard on a stout grey courser.

Leaving behind any decorum, Ursula ran out to greet her youngest brother.

"What has happened?" She reached for his hand, gripping it hard out of fear when she saw how pale and strained he looked. "Tell me, Geoffrey."

"Mother has been dismissed from Princess Mary's household. Our brother, Lord Montagu, is in the Tower. Everyone is being questioned."

She gasped. "Henry arrested? On what charge?"

Geoffrey shook his head. "Thankfully he is only under investigation. There is no charge brought against him."

She felt her breath return. "And the Duke? Is there news?"

Geoffrey dismounted, looking past her to Henry who had appeared in the doorway. "He is to be tried by a jury of his peers. The date hasn't been set yet."

"And the charge against him?" Henry asked, walking forward, his posture stiff.

"Treason."

Ursula's knees threatened to buckle, but she held herself together. The three of them glanced away from each other. They knew what this meant. The Cardinal had won and would bring down the Duke of Buckingham.

"I should tell my mother," Henry said after a long silence. "We must prepare ourselves for the worst possible news."

"But we shall pray for the King's mercy," Ursula said, placing a hand on his shoulder.

"The King has waited for this day for a long time. He won't let my father go, not now he has him in his claws."

"Henry," she snapped. "Is it right you should question his judgment like this?"

Aware of the listening ears of servants who might report on them, he shook his head. "You misunderstand me. The King is a paragon of justice and virtue. He will see that justice is done." But the look he gave her told a different story. He pushed past her and disappeared into the house.

"Will you stay the night?" Ursula asked, turning back to Geoffrey.

He shook his head, patting his horse's neck. "I am to ride back to Warblington without delay. We shall rest at an inn along the road."

She didn't blame him. It was better to sleep under a stranger's roof than under a traitor's.

When he embraced her, he pressed a slip of parchment into her hands. "Take care of yourself, sister. May God watch over you."

"And you as well."

She watched him go with a heavy heart. In the privacy of her room she read the letter from her mother urging her to take every precaution. Anything that might incriminate them should be destroyed. Ursula fed this scrap of love and hope into the flame, lest her mother be accused of conspiring with the Duke of Buckingham.

Not long after Geoffrey's arrival, a deputation of the King's men arrived and tore Thornbury apart. The servants were questioned, as was Henry. The account books were taken away and the household left in shambles.

They waited on tenterhooks for news. Surely the King would pardon the Duke. They were cousins after all.

The one piece of good news was that her brother was released from prison. The Pole family was still under suspicion and banished from court, but they had their freedom.

Henry's hopes were raised by the news. "Surely the King will pardon my father now and set him free."

Ursula remained tight-lipped. Her brother had never said a single word against King Henry, yet he had been punished nonetheless. Perhaps this was just a show of strength by the King to remind everyone of his power.

"He will have seen the error of his ways and will repent. In the future, he will be more careful," Henry said, as though he was debating before the jury.

Again, Ursula didn't have the heart to reply and sat there mutely as he went on making promises and assurances.

Lady Eleanor shut herself away in her rooms, unable or unwilling to see any of them. It was left to Ursula to try to hold the family together.

Merchants and servants still had to be paid. One day she ventured to the office designated for the chancellor. She pored over the records, seeing if she could find the sums of money she would need to pay their debts. Would there be enough in the treasury to keep the household running over the winter?

For the first time it hit her that they might not have enough funds to cover their expenses. What would they do?

She tapped her finger on the parchment. Surely the gowns and jewels she had collected over the years could be sold off.

They would get through this, or at the very least, she had to ensure they wouldn't starve.

In May, one month after his arrest, Edward Stafford, Duke of Buckingham, was beheaded on Tower Hill.

For the crime of mere boastful words, he paid with his life. Even the torture of his servants couldn't reveal evidence he ever intended or was planning to take action against King Henry.

It didn't matter in the end, for the King was determined to make an example of him.

As the family was plunged into mourning, and dealing with unconfirmed reports, further news arrived from London. Following his death, the Duke was attainted. All his lands and property were forfeit to the Crown.

The news sent Henry into a spiral of depression. Ursula listened numbly as her mother-in-law read the letter from the Council.

When Ursula's mother had arranged her marriage, she had paid dearly for the privilege of her daughter one day becoming the Duchess of Buckingham. Given the benefits of the connection, it had been a risk the Countess of Salisbury had been willing to take.

She had gambled and lost.

Through no fault of his own, Ursula's husband, Henry Stafford, would not become Duke of Buckingham. Instead, he and his family would now become dependent on the goodwill of their extended relatives.

News of the catastrophe spread quickly among their relations. However, Ursula, Henry and Lady Eleanor were left to weather the storm of uncertainty alone. No one wished to associate themselves with the family of a convicted traitor, lest suspicion fall upon them. The King was in a foul mood. Rumours from London claimed he was laid low by a sickness that kept him confined to his bed.

How ironic would it be if the King were to die now? The Duke's ambitions might have come to pass after all. But he was dead, and the King was being tended to by the best doctors in England.

Slowly and secretly, messages of support began to arrive from several quarters.

"My lady, you are wanted in the courtyard," a servant said.

Ursula looked up from the desk, trying to work out the funds the family would need once the King's men took hold of everything.

"Who is it?"

"A merchant, my lady."

Ursula scoffed. "Send him away. We have no money for frivolities."

"He was insistent he speak to you." The servant was just as annoyed as she was.

"Very well," she said, getting to her feet.

Outside, a humble merchant dressed in plain black

clothing was waiting by his cart. He bowed to her when he saw her.

"What can I help you with?" Ursula asked. "You must have heard that the Duke of Buckingham was executed. We have no funds to purchase trinkets from you."

His expression was grim, and he kept glancing at the maid who accompanied her. "Nevertheless, my lady, perhaps you would like to see my wares before sending me away."

Something in his expression alerted Ursula, and she agreed.

He walked round to the back of the cart and flung off the cover to show her the bolts of wool beneath. "You will want to examine the black, my lady. It is of especially fine quality and given you are in mourning, you might find it useful." He pointed to one in particular.

Gingerly, Ursula reached for it. Her eyes caught sight of parchment rolled up within it.

"Are you certain it would be suitable for those in mourning?" she said, aware for the first time that her maid might report on her.

The merchant nodded. "Yes, feel the quality of the cloth. There is no finer weave in all of England." He pulled out the bolt, and Ursula managed to grab hold of the letter and slip it into the large sleeve of her gown. Her heart was racing as she turned towards him.

"I can see you are correct about the fabric, but unfortunately I have no funds to pay you with. I hope you shall find me another time."

"Of course, my lady. Thank you for taking the time to speak with me." He bowed, doffing his cap. It was then she caught sight of the familiar pin on his lapel. The emblem of Saint Andrew, the very same one she had sent Lady Elizabeth when she had heard about her difficult birth.

She backed away slowly and returned to the house, ignoring the urge to watch him go.

Once she was back inside, she walked past her solar and went straight to her bedroom.

"Alice, I have a headache. Please see if the cook will prepare me a tisane." She made a great show of lying on a divan before the fire and rubbing at her temple.

Her maid left, leaving Elizabeth free to open her letter. Her heart swelled at the sight of the familiar handwriting.

Lady Elizabeth, forbidden from writing to or seeing her family by her husband, had found a way to defy him.

Ursula kissed the letter, her wet eyes with tears.

Dearest Sister,

I am grieved to hear of your troubles. As you may know by now my father-in-law sat on the jury that tried my father. We had not expected the King's wrath to fall so heavily upon you after he was executed. I can only imagine what you must be feeling but at least you and Henry will have each other.

Ursula scoffed at that, while at the same time wishing desperately it was true.

I am sending this letter by my manservant who is loyal to me, disguised as a merchant. He has been paid handsomely for accomplishing this task. As I am pressed for time, I must be quick. Beyond offering you support and my love, I am powerless to do anything to help you. My husband is a tyrant if there ever was one. I urged him to speak to the King against the attainder and — well you can imagine what his fury was like. Please look after yourselves and your precious little son. Thank God he is too young to understand what is happening. I trust that in time justice will be done and in the meantime I will pray for you. One day I hope to be able to do more than just offer you kind words.

Your loving sister,

E.

Reading her kind words and affirmations of her continued love, Ursula felt invigorated. Yes, she wished Elizabeth could have helped them in a more substantial way, but she was grateful beyond words. Before her maid could return she tucked the letter away at the bottom of her chests.

It wasn't long before the King's administrators came to Thornbury and began taking an account of all the goods. Watching these men pick through their possessions made Ursula feel sick. But it was a reminder that nothing was theirs anymore.

Would the King take pity on them and return their holdings?

For the moment it appeared he was not in a generous mood.

Her jewels, the expensive gowns of cloth of gold and the decadent red velvet harness Henry had purchased for her horse were packed away and sent to London.

At least the King's men were not cruel. Under Wolsey's direction they were to ensure the Duke's widow and son were not left empty handed.

It was agreed that Ursula would retain the dower property her mother had settled upon her, and the goods she had brought with her. With this in mind, Ursula followed the commissioners around, ensuring they took nothing that had been hers before her marriage.

One of these commissioners was Master Adrian Smith, and today he was determined to sort through the tapestries, which had been gathered and laid out in the long gallery.

Ursula followed after him, trying to maintain a sense of dignity as she watched over his shoulder.

"That tapestry was part of my dowry," she said, pointing to one of the finer ones. The gold thread in the piece alone would fetch a handsome price.

He considered it, then shot a look at a clerk who was following behind them with a writing desk. "Is there any mention of this tapestry in the household account?"

Ursula had a ready answer. "You'll find it listed in the inventory that came with my dowry."

The middle-aged man eyed her but decided it wasn't worth arguing. "Very well, Lady Ursula. I will be sure to cross-check it with the other records."

"I understand," she said, wrenching her hands together. Her nerves were mounting with each passing moment. "I am grateful for the Cardinal's kindness and understanding."

Adrian Smith nodded. "Set that one aside," he directed another servant.

The small triumph was dwarfed by the embarrassment she felt.

Henry was lost in a cloud of misery and regret. He couldn't bear to watch his hopes and dreams being taken away like this, so it was left to her to claw back as much as she could.

She didn't care if she had to stoop to grovelling and arguing over something as insignificant as silver spoons. Ursula and her husband faced a dismal future. All they had to their names were a few acres of farmland that brought in one hundred pounds per annum, assuming the harvest was good; some clothes and jewels, and items like this tapestry, which she would quickly sell to pay the servants' wages and put food on the table.

The Cardinal in his wisdom had directed that the family be allowed one horse apiece, and that carts and oxen should be provided for their use. They were given until the end of the month to leave Thornbury.

Given the circumstances, it was generous of him, but where would they go? They had no home to retreat to. Not even a miserable little cottage.

Ursula had written to her mother and brother hoping they could think of a solution. Surely one of them had a spare house Ursula and her family could use.

She bit her lip because she knew her mother was tight-fisted when it came to money, and might not be willing to accommodate them. Henry, already on edge, would feel slighted by everything and anything they were offered.

With this in mind Ursula wrote another letter, in secret, to the Cardinal. She begged him to intercede with the King on Henry's behalf, reminding the Cardinal that even the Bible said the sins of the father ought not to pass on to the son.

As of yet, it had gone unanswered, cementing her shame.

She had not found it in her heart to tell Henry what she had done, knowing he would never forgive her.

The only peace and tranquillity to be found in the household was in Harry's nursery. To soothe the anxieties of the nursemaid and wet nurse, Ursula had bribed them each with gold hairpins and the promise that before all other expenses, their wages would be paid. When she wasn't holding her son or marvelling at how he had grown, she prayed in the chapel for God's intercession.

Ursula ran out into the courtyard, the folds of her gown billowing around her.

"Lady Eleanor!" she called out to her mother-in-law, who was mounted on a dark bay gelding. Two guards studied the cart loaded with goods, checking the ties were in place. Dawn had just arrived and the household was still rising. In the quiet of the early morning, Ursula's words echoed around the palace courtyard.

Her mother-in-law reined in her horse and turned to face her. Ursula was taken aback by the cool detachment in her eyes.

"What are you doing?" Ursula asked.

"I see politeness has left you," Lady Eleanor sniffed.

"You are leaving." Ursula bit her lower lip when the older woman didn't deny it. "How could you?"

Lady Eleanor straightened, her gaze fixed on the gatehouse. "There's nothing for me here. I am returning to my brother's house. I am sure in due course another marriage will be arranged for me."

"How can you say that? Your son and your grandson are here. I know your husband's passing—"

"His execution," she corrected. "He was a traitor. I won't remain here and pretend to mourn for a man who doesn't deserve my tears. Look what he has brought down upon us." She gave a wave of her hand. "I will always love my son, but I cannot stay a moment longer. Nor can I help either of you."

"Your family could—"

"They won't. As far as they're concerned, it is bad enough that I am returning to them. They don't want the shadow of my husband's crime to fall upon them. Henry is a grown man. He will make his own way in the world. He doesn't need his mother."

Ursula stepped away, unable to comprehend her ruthlessness.

"I am sorry this has happened. But I must think of my own future now." Lady Eleanor's grip tightened on her reins.

The way she kept repeating the phrase made Ursula think she wasn't quite convinced herself. Lady Eleanor must have been acting against every instinct, every fibre of her being, by leaving like this. And she had chosen to slink off at daybreak without a proper farewell — like a coward.

Yet for all that she had made her choice. She could've stayed.

There was no more to say.

Ursula's throat tightened as she retreated back into the house. How would she tell Henry?

In Lady Eleanor's abandoned room, a letter was waiting on her desk. Glancing around the room there was nothing left behind besides the feather bed and the solid oak bed frame.

She glanced at the letter and saw Henry's name scrawled underneath the seal. Picking it up she thought about destroying it, but instead found herself carrying it to his room.

Henry's valet was outside, sleeping on a pallet bed. Henry's desire to be alone had grown.

She knocked on the heavy door and heard shuffling behind it. She waited a few moments then knocked again. This time the door swung open and Henry stepped out, his eyes groggy.

"Wh-at? Ursula? What are you doing here?"

"Your mother has left."

He gaped at her, and she took advantage of the moment of confusion to push her way into his room.

The stale smell of sweat and unwashed sheets assaulted her senses. She strode to the window and opened the shutters to let in fresh air before spinning around to face her husband.

"It's time you returned to the world."

He scowled at her, but then all at once his shoulders slumped forward. "So she has left?"

"Yes. Just a few minutes ago. You might be able to catch her on the road if you take a fast horse." She motioned towards the door.

"No," he said, pinching the bridge of his nose. "It's in her nature to flee. Her leaving tells me it's time for us to go as well."

"And where are we going, Henry?" she asked, unable to hide her irritation with him.

"My sister Katherine has prevailed upon her husband, the Earl of Westmorland, to take us in. She reminded him that he owes our family fealty for having raised him and protected his earldom. We will live there in comfort until we can regroup. Perhaps your mother will reply to your letters." He paused, eyeing her. "Or the Cardinal."

She felt her cheeks turn red but kept her head high. "I did what I had to do. You shall not reproach me."

He raked a hand through his hair. "Indeed I won't. I only pray for your success. From now on we must make our own way in the world. It's a daunting task going from lord to beggar."

She gave him a grim smile. "You'll find a way to manage."

"Together."

Ursula held his gaze. "Together." Fresh hope sprung within her as she felt the strength of his hold and knew she could rely on him to support her.

He solemnised their oath with a kiss, from which she pulled away, laughing. "But first a bath."

"Read it again," Ursula said, sitting on the edge of the bed as her husband, happy to obey her command, began again.

"*His Majesty King Henry Tudor, at the request and deliberation with the Privy Council, has granted you the manors of Staffordshire and Shropshire. Henceforth, these manors and their lands shall hereby be returned to your possession and control...*"

Ursula's heart soared. "And you said summer would never come." She glanced around the room; soon she'd have a home of her own to decorate. The Earl of Westmorland had been true to his word and they were lodged in comfortable guestrooms at Brancepeth Castle. It had been lovely to have Katherine's company, but they never stopped feeling like guests.

Henry grinned at her. "I thought you wanted me to read you the letter."

Springing to her feet she giggled. "You've read the most important part. Henry, I cannot believe it."

He smiled, but his exuberance was not as high as her own. "What's wrong?"

"The vultures have picked over the carcass of my father's lands and now we are left with the bones. I worry about the state of these manors. We have neither the funds to build anew nor repair."

"We shall make do. My mother has paid out the rest of my dowry to you and we have the income from my farm-land. With some economising we shall manage." She grabbed his hand, squeezing it lightly so he would meet her eyes. "This is only the first step in our recovery. My mother managed it why can't we?"

"Your mother is half in exile herself," he pointed out.

"For now. The Queen sent her a New Year's gift. It's a sign that the King is softening towards us. Why are you so determined to be miserable?"

"I've been far too optimistic in the past. But you are right, this is a step forward. The King has been in a giving mood ever since the Pope granted him the title Defender of the Faith."

Ursula released him and wandered over to her wooden chest, throwing back the lid and pulling out one of her fine velvet kirtles. It was a beautiful deep blue that she had embroidered with white roses.

"Let's hope his good mood lasts longer than his alliance with France," she said, pulling out the matching foresleeves. Then she stopped. "Henry, with this gift of manors you shall have to muster a retinue of men and ride out to war."

He nodded gravely. "The King's generosity is poorly timed. I shall have to go to France with the army rather than see us settled in our new home. It would've been nice to see the first harvest being brought in."

Fear gripped her by the throat and her eyes widened. "But what if something happens to you?"

He took her in his arms and kissed her brow. "Then you shall have to manage Harry's lands until he comes of age. Or perhaps your mother will arrange another great marriage for you."

"Ha. After how the last one turned out I think I shall consider taking the veil," she said.

"With your love of finery?"

"I've changed my mind. Go to France." She let out an exasperated huff. "Besides, I've learned to live without finery." She laid a hand on the kirtle. "This is the finest thing I own now. Two years ago I would've thought this was a suitable dress for my maid."

"We've all changed."

As though on cue, their little son toddled into the room, his nurse hot on his heels.

"I apologise, my lord," the nurse said, pink in the face. "He escaped."

Henry laughed, picking up the little toddler and tossing him into the air.

"Up. Up," Harry said in his broken speech.

Ursula's heart swelled at the sight of father and son. Harry would celebrate his second birthday soon. Of all of them, he had changed the most. Growing more with each passing day, he was talking now and impressed her with how much he could absorb.

Confined as they were to the charity of their family and friends, Ursula didn't know how they would hire tutors for him, but was resolved to teach him herself. She also wished there was another child he could play with. Despite their tight funds she wished there was another child on the way, but as yet there were no signs.

"What do you say, Harry? Would you like to learn to manage a manor?"

Harry squealed as his father tickled him.

"Good boy." Henry kissed his forehead and set him down.

Harry moved about the room, his eyes catching sight of the candlestick on a table. He made his way towards it. His nurse was faster and swept him up before he could cause any harm, saying, "I'll take him to play in the gardens."

"And I shall join you shortly," Ursula said. Then turning to Henry she said, "We need to start planning for the move."

The Earl was happy to provide them with everything they could need for their journey. A small army of carts, horses and guards arrived to safely escort them to Staffordshire.

Ursula watched as their meagre possessions were loaded onto the waiting carts, pleased with the progress they were making. The journey would take a few days and she didn't want anything to go missing. They couldn't afford it.

"I shall have to write to your sister Elizabeth, to let her know when we've arrived," Ursula said as Henry came to stand beside her, hands on his hips.

"Do you think the great Countess will deign to visit us at our lowly manor?"

She rolled her eyes. "Staffordshire sounds promising

enough. Your man said it's in good repair. And Elizabeth is eager to come. She would've visited us here if you hadn't told her to stay away."

"I didn't want to hear you two chattering away like birds."

"Then I shall tell her to keep me company while you are in France."

He shook his head. "As you please."

That evening Katherine held a banquet in their honour, and Ursula wondered if they would ever be able to repay them for their generosity.

The only other option they had been given was to live with her mother at Warblington. Compared to Ursula's strict mother, Katherine was by far a better host. In the year they stayed with her she never once made them feel unwelcome, and Ursula loved her all the more for it.

As they travelled into Staffordshire, the route took them past the castle that had been part of Henry's inheritance. His gaze was grim as he stared at the stone façade, but then he determinately turned away and directed their company towards a smaller road. Even though the castle was his ancestral seat, it had been an age since Henry had visited Staffordshire. Twice they had to stop to ask for directions to the manor.

At last they came to the hill with the grove of chestnuts.

What sort of state would their new home be in? Ursula's anxiety peaked as they turned onto the overgrown path. Trying her best to appear confident, she glanced behind her to smile at Harry, who was cuddling in his nurse's arms.

Stafford Manor came into view and Ursula breathed a sigh of relief. The two-story timber-framed house with its tiled roof was nestled before an overgrown garden. She said a prayer of thanks that the windows appeared to be intact.

"Here it is, our new home," Henry said, urging his horse onward.

There was no one to greet them. The meagre staff they had brought with them would have to suffice until they could hire more. Ursula wondered if there was a cook among them.

Henry jumped down from his horse with a grunt and pushed open the wide door. He smiled encouragingly before disappearing inside.

Ursula was helped down from the cart. "Wait here while we see where we can set up Harry with his own room," she said to the nurse.

Above the doorway, the painted Stafford family crest had faded with time and neglect. The walls were chipped and would need to be resurfaced before the winter months, when the chill would seep into every crack of the house.

Following Henry, Ursula stepped into a wide hallway. Doors on either side led to an office, and a dining hall that was attached to a small parlour. Ursula headed for the stairs. They creaked as she climbed, hoisting up her skirts.

Henry stepped out from one of the rooms. His smile was strained as he said, "This shall be our bedroom. It's not much."

"It's more than we had," Ursula reminded him gently. "We can make some improvements too."

The room was small, but the wood-panelled walls were still beautiful. Together they explored the other rooms, finding at least two others in good repair. Harry could have use of those, and there was plenty of room for the servants they had brought with them.

The timber beams in the dining room were carved with interweaving vines that drew the eye. The furniture left behind by the King's men was simple and functional. Some pieces were in need of repair, but Ursula reminded herself to be grateful. Besides, what could they do about it? They couldn't purchase new furniture.

Most troubling of all was the empty larder. They would need to fill it if they were going to make it through the winter.

Ursula felt her throat close up as those dark, spiralling thoughts crept in again. She envisioned her son starving, without a crust of bread to his name. Resolutely she shook her head, forcing such images away. She was determined to learn. People managed on far less.

Ursula spied Henry entering the kitchen. "There's a lot of work to do," she said, "but I'm pleasantly surprised this isn't some shepherd's cottage."

He wrapped an arm around her waist and pulled her close, burying his head in the nape of her neck. He breathed in her comforting scent and said, "I would trade this house for an ounce of your optimism."

She pulled away so she could look into his blue eyes. "Given how little you seem to value this house, that is not much of a compliment."

❧

Henry had very little time at Stafford House before he had to leave for France.

"I am to travel to Calais and join the Duke of Suffolk there."

"I assume you'll have to pay your own travel expenses?" Ursula sighed, brushing her hands on her apron. She'd been busy the past few days, making preserves from the fruit picked from their apple trees. They had hired a cook and scullery maid, but in an effort to economise Ursula took over some of the seasonal tasks. Preserves, and tinctures made from the plants in the herb garden, would ensure the household not only had food in the winter, but also medicine.

"Naturally," Henry said. "But the King is paying us generously, so perhaps we can have the house re-plastered before the winter."

"We'll manage."

Their list of projects was ever expanding while their resources were not. However, they were better off than they were a few months ago, and with every successful harvest more money trickled in. From her mother, the remainder of her dowry paid the upfront cost of the staff they would need, and would enable them to get a better foothold in the region.

Clearing away the overgrowth had revealed the remains of two knot gardens, and a herb garden, which was still flourishing. The fence around the paddock had been repaired and their two horses were grazing on the green grass.

A temporary barn had been erected, but if they wished to keep a few pigs and cows for meat and milk then they would need to set aside funds to pay for a larger, permanent structure. Perhaps all this careful planning and consideration was unnecessary and the King would grant them more lands, but as they had learned, nothing in life was guaranteed. They'd been humbled, but Ursula felt they were strong enough to overcome this adversity.

Henry had surprised her these last few months. After his father's death he had been at a loss for what to do. Now he had matured, setting aside his gambling and leisurely pastimes. He embraced the responsibility of caring for his family and providing for them. He spent long days out visiting the farms and the tenants, ensuring everything was in proper working order. Knowing he'd be called to fight in France, he hired a team of administrators to collect rents and ensure the harvest was brought in. Ursula was thankful beyond measure. Knowing she could rely on him gave her confidence for their future.

The day before he left, they strolled through the yard and down the gravel path overlooking the meadow and farmland beyond, watching the setting sun as it painted the sky in hues of purple and gold.

Ursula rested her head on his shoulder. "Come back to me."

Henry took a deep breath. "Since you demand it of me."

She jabbed a finger into his side, which made him laugh.

In December, Elizabeth found her way to Stafford House.

It was unsuitable for such a grand lady to visit a poor

house like theirs. In her anxiety, Ursula took special care with her gown and headdress.

She waited by the front door as her sister-in-law rode up the cobbled pathway. Their one groom ran forward with a block to help her dismount.

Ursula hoped Elizabeth wouldn't regret her decision to visit. The family was close, but until this moment they had kept in contact by letter, or during visits to Warblington, when her mother invited the extended family.

What would Elizabeth think of their new home? The manor must appear to be little more than a hovel. To her credit, she showed no signs of discomfort as she approached, arms outstretched.

Ursula began to curtsey, but Elizabeth would have none of it and flung her arms around her neck. "It's been ages. How have you been?" she said, glancing around.

"I've been well. Missing Henry every day. The Duke of Suffolk keeps his men busy raiding the French countryside, but no move's been made to attack Paris. Don't let me keep you out here. Come inside." Ursula ushered her through the door.

Elizabeth had brought two chambermaids, a manservant, and a retinue of guards. Ursula hoped she could house them all in comfort for the duration of their stay.

"I don't recall ever coming to Stafford House, but I can see the foundation is strong and it's a pretty manor," Elizabeth said, as she was led into the parlour.

Here, Ursula's work as a housekeeper was visible. The tapestries that hadn't been sold were hung with care, and there was a portrait of Henry above the mantel. She offered

Elizabeth a platter of candied fruits arranged in the shape of a flower, and urged her to take a seat.

It wasn't long before the two women shrugged off their awkwardness and fell into their old friendship. Ursula might not have the funds to purchase the finest velvets, but she knew enough about the latest daring fashions to share her opinion.

"Half the Queen's ladies are wearing their dresses cut low enough that everyone can see their breasts," Elizabeth said.

Surely she was exaggerating, but Ursula didn't voice her disbelief. She loved hearing of Elizabeth's adventures at court. There was a never-ending stream of intrigue, petty gossip and fights. Given her quiet life in the country, this had her on the edge of her seat.

"You won't have heard this piece of gossip," Elizabeth said, leaning forward. "The King has a new bastard. A girl — they've called her Catherine. Could you imagine the audacity of such a thing? It's a slap in the Queen's face."

"And the mother?"

"Mary Boleyn. The King hasn't acknowledged the child officially, but he gifted Mary an allowance. She's to be known as Catherine Carey. My husband thinks he can rise in the King's esteem by offering up women of our family for him to bed. It's despicable."

Elizabeth took a sip of her honeyed ale before launching into a tirade about the immorality of mistresses. It was a touchy subject, as her husband was keeping a mistress and treating her far better than Elizabeth. And by all accounts, Elizabeth was a faultless wife. She'd given her husband a nursery full of children, the most recent only this year. She was devout and loyal to him, or had been, but none of this had not stopped her husband from mistreating her.

Now that her father was dead and she was no longer the daughter of a duke, he felt safe insulting her.

Despite Elizabeth's vibrant personality and strength, it was clear she was suffering. Her cheeks were hollow; her skin had lost its healthy pink glow and had become sallow.

"Stop looking at me like that."

Ursula gave a start and blinked. "I'm sorry."

"It's I who should be pitying you, not the other way around," Elizabeth said, but she sunk into her seat and stared at the ceiling.

Ursula knew her well enough not to take anything she said to heart. "Was your son's birth hard on you?" It was common for a difficult birth to leave a lasting impact on a woman.

Elizabeth's lips pinched tight as though she was fighting to hold back the words.

"You can tell me," Ursula said. "There's no one here to overhear you."

The corner of Elizabeth's lips twisted into an insincere smile. "We fought. He came to see the baby once it was born and matters got out of hand..."

Ursula's stomach coiled unpleasantly.

"I — I should've stopped. I threw a candlestick at him and he grabbed me by my hair and —" She stopped, unable to go on. Ursula gaped. "Anyway it was horrible." Elizabeth cleared her throat. "But I told him if he tries to return to my bed, I'll kill him. My threats must have worked because he hasn't. We live apart now. I see my children as often as I can, but he is eager to keep them away from me."

Heartbroken for her friend, Ursula remained silent for a long time. "In time, perhaps, you will reach an accord." She was grasping at straws.

Elizabeth waved away her concerns. "I will have none of that. This is my lot in life. Please don't tell Henry; it will only make him feel more powerless that he cannot do anything for me. Or even worse, he might invite more trouble to his door if he decides to confront him."

"Someone ought to."

Ursula's inner turmoil and regret was reflected in Elizabeth's eyes. The two women turned to regard the flickering flames in the fireplace.

"Tell me more about the pageant you saw on Shrove Tuesday at court. Was Chateau Vert as magnificent as my brother Arthur claims?"

They were invited to Warblington to celebrate Easter with Ursula's family. The wheel of fortune was turning again. Her mother received the news that she would be reappointed as Princess Mary's governess. This show of royal favour thrilled lady Margaret.

In the four years since the Duke's execution, the King's anger towards the family had melted away. Ursula's brother Lord Montagu was invited back to court, and was present when King Henry met with Emperor Charles. The French campaign had come to nothing, but Ursula's husband's good service had not gone unnoticed. Further lands were restored to them, including the drafty Staffordshire Castle. They left Stafford Manor and moved to the larger accommodations, but Ursula found she missed the smaller house with its cosy rooms.

Harry was now a precocious boy of four, and Ursula had hired a tutor for him. He had a knack for numbers, but to the dismay of both parents he always found ways of getting into trouble.

Ursula had still not conceived again. Between Henry's frequent absences from home and other duties, they were often apart, yet she couldn't help but worry.

"You should be counting your blessings," her mother said, a sharp edge of reprimand in her voice. "Think of the Queen and her suffering. Think how far you have come. Do not wallow in self-pity."

"I am well aware I have much to be thankful for, Lady Mother," Ursula said, unable to keep from answering back. "I was merely expressing a desire—" She noted her mother's thunderous expression and stopped herself. "Of course, you are right."

Lady Margaret patted her daughter's hands. "When you have lived as long as I have, you will realise that wishing for things to happen is a waste of time."

Later that day as they weaved crowns of flowers, her sister-in-law, Lady Katherine, surprised Ursula by agreeing with the Countess.

"I thought you'd be more sympathetic," said Ursula.

Lady Katherine laughed. "Oh I am." She put a hand to her belly. "Look at me. My waist disappears a little further with every child I carry in my womb. There's never a moment's peace at my house. But now, in all seriousness — I am sorry you have been unable to conceive. But wishful thinking will only make you miserable." She stopped as a mischievous grin spread across her face. "You must take action."

Ursula burst into uncontrollable laughter. "Now that is good advice."

"But not until after Lent is over," Lady Katherine reminded her with a sheepish grin.

On Easter Day, they attended Mass at Lady Margaret's chapel. As with everything in Ursula's mother's house, it was lavishly decorated. There were stained-glass windows, beautiful altar clothes and a crucifix made of gold.

All the lights had been extinguished in the chapel and only now, on Easter Day, did the priest remove the host from the sepulchre to symbolise that Christ had risen.

With that, the season of Lent was over and the large family party returned to the house, where Lady Margaret had arranged a great banquet. The tables in the dining hall were sumptuously laid, and each family member dined on silver plates and drank from Venetian wine glasses. Servants carried in delicacies, mutton, venison, sparrows, and pies, followed by delicious pastries and cakes.

Ursula gave a contented sigh as she sipped at the fine wine from Bordeaux. She didn't think she could eat another morsel.

Looking around the table she marvelled at how much they had all changed. Her elder brother, Lord Montagu, was no longer an untried youth. There was an air of gravitas about him as he inclined his head to listen to what their mother was saying. A politician through and through, he was attentive to those around him and circumspect in his behaviour.

He was also observant. Ursula's study of him did not go unnoticed for long, and he flashed her a quick smile.

Further down the table, Arthur was laughing merrily at something Geoffrey had said. His manner was light and easy going, as it had ever been. But he had become a soldier.

His sturdy frame and height spoke of his strength. At court he was a favourite of the King for his skill at jousting. In France he had been knighted for his bravery on the battlefield.

Reginald was not here, but he too was succeeding within the Church. The King was pleased with him, and happy to pay for him to study in Italy.

At twenty-one, Geoffrey was still young but was increasingly unsure of his position within the family. Their mother spoiled him, ensuring he had everything he could desire and providing him with clothes fit for a lord. Ursula wondered what her mother planned to do with her fourth son, but she was sure some place would be secured for him, if not at court then in Parliament.

That only left her.

In many ways she had become the failure of the family. Her great prospects had come to nothing, and she was the poor relation to be pitied and helped out of charity. In the past, her pride would have prevented her from accepting their help; she would've felt insulted. But now she welcomed all the help she could get.

At her side she could sense Henry growing uneasy. To him this was a reminder of all they had lost. Just five years ago a banquet of this size and magnitude had been par for the course. He was hiding his discomfort well, but having lived with him for six years she could read his emotions far better than anyone else at this table.

"Husband, we shall be home soon. We might as well take advantage of this time to relax and fatten up for the season." Her tone was light-hearted, but his lips thinned into a grimace.

After dinner, the ladies withdrew to Lady Margaret's private solar to sit by the fire and talk, while the men retreated to another room to play cards and discuss business.

Lady Jane, Lord Montagu's wife, was leaning back on a couch. She had recently been churched and was still recovering from the labour, even though it had been months.

She'd given her husband two daughters already, and this third pregnancy had produced another. The failure to bear her husband an heir was weighing heavily on her. She'd always been serious, but now, even as they went around sharing family news and stories about their children, her smiles were empty.

Ursula knew that her brother was far too kind to ever think of reproaching his wife. But as Ursula watched her mother she couldn't help wondering if the pressure was coming from a different quarter altogether. Every time Jane spoke or laughed, Lady Margaret's pinched expression would turn on her, and she would fall silent.

The Countess of Salisbury was a harsh woman who expected perfection in all her children. For most of her childhood, Ursula had escaped her tough demands, as she'd been left in the care of a governess and tutor while Lady Margaret was at court. Yet she vividly remembered how the household would be on tenterhooks every time her mother visited. Ursula would walk on eggshells, afraid any tiny mistake would result in stern admonishment from her all-powerful mother. On one occasion, when she'd spilled ink on her gown, she'd been so terrified she'd hidden in one of the store rooms. It had taken a lot of coaxing by her governess to come out.

Years ago, she had seen Jane as something of a rival, envious she would live with Ursula's family while Ursula would have to move out. She'd taken to gloating over every little triumph, including her own betrothal to a future duke. Now she wished she had taken more care to get to know her.

Arthur's wife, the other Jane, turned her attention to Ursula. "You didn't tell us your mother-in-law remarried." The statement was innocent enough, but for the sly look in her eye.

Ursula's breath caught in her throat. "I didn't know."

"I am surprised," she said, attempting to sound sincere. "Perhaps Lady Eleanor wrote to her son and he did not tell you. Still, I find the whole business unnatural. How could she have abandoned you like that?"

With one stroke she had reminded all those in the room of Ursula's fall from grace, painting her as someone who ought to be pitied. But Arthur's wife seemed to have forgotten that Lady Katherine was Lady Eleanor's daughter too. Katherine was wringing her hands in her lap, her eyes shooting daggers at the thoughtless woman. However, she was far too meek to speak out.

Ursula, more adept at concealing her emotions and braving any storm, asked coolly, "Who has she married?"

"Sir John Audley."

The name was familiar, but she couldn't place it.

"I wish her every joy. The Percys have enjoyed a string of marriages lately. I know Henry Percy has finally married Mary Talbot, though he didn't wish to. Strange, isn't it? Usually it is the bride who is reluctant."

"You are well informed," Arthur's wife said, surprised.

Ursula's lips curled at the snide comment. She'd succeeded in showing everyone that though they might be impoverished and in disgrace, she wasn't ignorant. She made a mental note to thank Elizabeth for keeping her abreast of the gossip.

Many ladies chuckled, and the conversation veered to speculating about what had happened.

"He fancied himself in love with some lowly peasant girl. Wanted to marry her," one lady said.

Another shook her head. "No, he heard that Mary Talbot was hideously scarred by smallpox."

"It wasn't a peasant girl," Lady Katherine interjected. She'd found her voice at last. "My husband says it was one of the ladies in the Queen's apartments. But regardless of his wishes, the match was unsuitable."

That set off a fresh round of questions, but it was Lady Katherine who was at the centre of the conversation.

Back in Staffordshire, Ursula and Henry were exhausted after the long journey. Harry was no longer easy to manage, and wouldn't sit still in the litter with his nurses.

"Perhaps we shall leave him at home next year," Henry said.

"Or we celebrate Easter on our own." Ursula rested her head against her pillow. It had been exciting to be among so many people and see her family again, but the underlying tension and competition simmering beneath the surface of every interaction was wearing.

Henry pulled her towards him. "I have something to speak to you about," he murmured.

Suddenly alert, she propped herself up on her elbows.

"I have been corresponding with Sir Thomas More. He has made some suggestions that I would be a fool not to listen to."

"Out with it, Henry. Don't force me to pry the information out of you."

"He has written that he would furnish me with a letter of recommendation so I might study law at Grey's Inn."

Ursula blinked. "You mean to become a lawyer?"

"You think it's beneath me."

"I would've thought *you* believed so. Have things become so desperate you wish to take on a trade?"

"I'm thinking of the opportunities that will come our way because of it. Look at Sir Thomas More and others who have risen in the King's favour for the services and advice they can provide. In the past my name alone would open doors for me, but obviously that's no longer an option."

She put a hand on his chest. "I understand."

"But something is bothering you. I hear the hesitation in your voice."

Ursula smiled to herself. When had he become so perceptive? Maybe he'd always been, but it was only in these recent years that he'd taken the trouble to really get to know her. "Studying at Grey's Inn will mean you will be away from home for a long time. That's what bothers me."

He laid his hand on hers. "Time will pass swiftly. I am not some immature young man. When I'm there I will keep my head down and study. I also promise to visit as often as I can."

Ursula let out a breath. "I support you. I just wish you didn't have to go."

"I don't have to leave right away. This could be months away. Assuming they even accept me."

"Don't be ridiculous; they will, and in the meantime we must make the most of the time we have," she said, leaning over and pressing her lips to his.

The summer heat was stifling. Ursula found relief under the shade of the chestnut trees. She sat on a blanket watching Harry run around. He would bring her back little treasures — rocks, and twigs that had fallen.

"Mama, look at this," he said, holding up a wriggling toad.

Ursula screamed. "Harry! Let that go at once."

He pouted, his little eyes scrunching up ready to bawl. Ursula, wise to his strategies, held up a finger. "None of that."

He let the toad go but was sad as he watched it disappear.

"Harry, you know better than to pick up every creature you come across, don't you? Come sit beside me and we can play a game."

He shook his head, determined to be miserable.

"Do as you please. I will lay back on this blanket and look up at dragons and castles."

That piqued his interest and he approached her pensively. She patted the spot beside her and he sat down.

"Those are clouds," he said.

"Only at first glance," she said. "Look carefully. See if you can tell me what shape that one is."

He was silent for a long time before he said, "A shield!"

"Very good." She smiled at him. He was blond and blue-eyed, the very image of his father, but his curls came from her and his stubborn disposition too. "Let's try another."

They sat beneath the oak, gazing up at the blue sky until his governess came looking for him. "The tutor is here, my lady."

"Very well." Ursula urged him to his feet.

"I don't want to go," Harry said, wrapping his arms around her and clinging to her tightly.

Gently, she pulled him off. "Be good and we can play again tomorrow. You need to learn your lessons."

"Why?" he asked, back to pouting.

"How else are you going to learn how to manage this estate? And just think, if you apply yourself you might become a courtier, increasing our nation's welfare."

"Like Uncle Montagu?"

"Exactly like him. He does very important work at court."

"And rides to war to protect us from the French," he half-shouted, making a slashing motion with his hand, as though battling an enemy.

What stories had he been listening to?

"We must take care of what we say," Ursula said. "Alliances can shift. Your father and I travelled with the King to France to sign a great peace treaty with the French king."

"But they are our enemy."

"At the moment," Ursula agreed. She smiled at the way

his brow furrowed as he tried to puzzle this out. "And this is exactly why I must send you to your tutors. It will help you to learn the ways of the world."

Reluctantly he left with the governess. She watched him go, her heart full of warmth. She lay back on the blanket, deciding she deserved a little rest before venturing to the dairy to check on the butter and cheese being made.

England had alternated her policies several times since the Field of the Cloth of Gold. One moment they were in alliance with Spain, and the next with France. It was difficult to predict which way the King's fancy would blow.

She turned her mind to Elizabeth, who was travelling through Staffordshire and would be stopping by. The accommodations Ursula could provide her with had improved in some regards. She would have a proper chamber with a fireplace of her own to keep her warm. The castle was still cold, as the repairs were moving slowly, entirely dependent on the excess profit they were able to squeeze out of their lands.

The previous year the crop had failed and the meagre harvest had barely fed them through the winter. They had borrowed money to pay for imported wheat.

Ursula's days were no longer consumed with idle pursuits. She had more in common with a merchant's wife than she did with Elizabeth, whose days revolved around hunting, embroidery and charitable works. She attended court functions, hosted banquets and celebrations, while Ursula worried over the quality of the cheese they sent to market.

It would be untrue to say she never felt envious of Elizabeth, but she appreciated her company, and the entertaining news she brought with her.

After a while, Ursula got up and dusted herself off. Her plain russet gown was starting to show signs of wear. She hoped there was some way to salvage it, because she thought the colour suited her.

In the dairy, she checked on the aging cheese and then supervised the dairy maid as she made the butter for their table. She directed her to add more salt to the mixture to increase the time it would keep in the larder. They had lost two of their milk cows to illness, and now butter was scarce in their household.

Inside she checked that the main chambers had been swept and that all was orderly. A shipment had just arrived from Henry at Grey's Inn. A servant had left the wooden chest in the corridor.

Prying open the lid, Ursula found herself staring at a number of books, all leather-bound and looking brand new. She frowned and picked up a volume. *Utopia* was embossed on the front; it was written by Sir Thomas More. Ursula wasn't sure what to make of her husband's new affection for the man.

Laying the book aside, she took up another. It was *Le Morte d'Arthur* in French, plus there were a few slim volumes of poetry by John Skelton.

She hoped these were gifts. Henry's love of books did not sit well with their diminished circumstances. These alone would have cost a tidy fortune. And to think she had abstained from ordering a new gown at Easter.

Bitterness entered her heart and she pushed it away.

Instead, she took the volumes and found a place for them in Henry's growing library.

As she entered, she sneezed at the overwhelming scent of old leather and dust in the air. Some of the wooden shelves were sagging, in need of repair and staining. The walls had been whitewashed but they were bare of any tapestry or decoration.

Finding room on his shelves, she slid the books into place. Ursula would have to speak to the housekeeper about airing out this musty room.

As she went to leave, she caught sight of the remains of two candles. There was still enough wax here that it could be saved and melted down to make new ones. Removing them from the candlesticks she slipped them into her pocket.

Seeing that all was in order, she donned an apron and went into the dining room. The rotten wood panelling had been removed the previous spring, and the walls were now plastered. She had set about painting them with Tudor roses and Fleur de Lys, alternating the colours in red and blue. It was a temporary solution, but one that gave purpose to her days.

As she dipped the brush into the paint, a wave of contentment washed over her.

CHAPTER 14

1525

"Staffordshire must be the quaintest county in all of England," Elizabeth said, as she came to a sudden stop.

Ursula pulled up her horse beside her. The bay mare was sure footed and strong, but not nearly as fast as Elizabeth's white hunter.

"You need not flatter me." Ursula swatted a fly buzzing round her face.

"After the stink of London, perhaps I am biased," Elizabeth threw over her shoulder. She dug her heels into her horse's flank and they flew down the hill towards the village.

Two guards followed behind, but kept their distance so the two women could have privacy.

Since her arrival, Elizabeth had been a bundle of energy and had yet to sit still. Her father-in-law had passed away a year ago, making her husband the third Duke of Norfolk. She was a duchess now, with even greater wealth and influence than before, but something was eating away at her. Ursula had come to learn that patience was the best way to handle her when she

177

was like this, so she attempted to keep up as Elizabeth woke early, explored the village market, hunted, and hawked. This was the fourth day of her visit and here they were, tiring their horses with another ride through the countryside. Ursula tried not to think about the tasks awaiting her back at the castle.

That evening she served her esteemed guest partridge, trout, and mutton. They ate off pewter plates, and drank the wine Elizabeth had brought with her.

"How is the Queen?" Ursula asked, believing it to be a safe topic.

"Why do you ask?" Elizabeth snapped, then remembering herself said, "I'm sorry. Forgive the outburst. The poor Queen." She gave a shake of her head.

"What has happened?" Ursula reached across the table and took her friend's hand in her own.

"Her courses have ceased," Elizabeth whispered. "By now, everyone knows."

So then, I am the last to know, thought Ursula.

"My husband is eager to use this to his advantage." Seeing Ursula's confusion, Elizabeth explained, "Mary Boleyn has given birth to another child, a boy. The King might be well disposed to rewarding the family as he plans to elevate Bessie Blount's son."

"The King will tire of her."

"Ha. Well, not to worry, the Duke has another Boleyn waiting to take her place." She shook her head again, and reached for her wineglass. "Everyone wonders what will happen. The throne is not secure."

"The King has the Princess Mary," Ursula pointed out.

"There would be a civil war again. No, the King is still

young and there is no reason to believe he will not father a son with another wife."

"The Queen is not ill, is she, God forbid?" The look Elizabeth gave her made her feel like a fool. "Oh, you mean that he will want to set her aside."

"She could take the veil. Then the King would be free to marry."

"Or he could legitimise Fitzroy. Why couldn't he just do that?"

Elizabeth shrugged. "Too many would contest it. He couldn't be sure that once he was gone, Fitzroy could hold the throne. It sickens me." She paused, taking a steadying breath. "My husband speaks of women as though they were disposable broodmares. Both the King and my husband have fickle memories. Do they forget the Queen is the daughter of Isabella of Castile? Do they forget how she defended the kingdom from the Scottish invasion? She is a devout woman and loving to her husband. Yet they want her to retire from her position simply because she has failed in this one thing? It's ridiculous."

"Are you sure of it?"

"No. But I can sense the way the wind is blowing. The King avoids her company unless the Spanish Ambassador is nearby. He mentioned his brother, Prince Arthur, recently. Spoke about how he doted on Queen Katherine. Perhaps Henry's beginning to doubt she was a virgin when he married her."

"Would that really be an issue? The marriage was blessed by the Church," Ursula said.

"We will see what happens next." Elizabeth had a

faraway look in her eyes. Ursula realised she was thinking of her own marriage, and her estranged husband.

"The Duke threatened to cut off my allowance if I didn't obey his wishes and retire to one of my dower estates. I fear that if he could, he would set me aside too. What would become of me then?"

"You have given him four healthy children. He wouldn't disinherit his sons, and from all you've told me, he dotes on his daughter too."

Elizabeth wiped at the corners of her eyes. "You are right. So instead he will hound me to my death. But I won't let him," she said, looking at Ursula as though she were making a solemn oath.

"You mentioned you were going to Kenilworth after visiting me."

"Yes, I am determined to ensure that the harlot he has installed in what should've been my rooms does not touch any of my jewels and gowns. And the children will be there too. It will be good to see them," she said as an afterthought.

Ursula nodded, remaining mute on the subject. For all Elizabeth's virtues, it was undeniable she was a distant mother. Her energy was eaten up by the constant bickering and fighting with her husband. This also explained some of her frantic energy. She was gathering her resources as though preparing to lay siege to Kenilworth. It was tragic it had come to this. Ursula was grateful Henry was a reason-able man she had come to respect and long for.

"I like the improvements you've been making to the castle," Elizabeth said, abruptly changing the topic.

It took Ursula a moment to recover. "I am thinking of having the ceiling painted blue. Like the one at Richmond, though of course we cannot have gold gilded beams and embellishments."

"A wonderful idea! I shall send you my painter. He does wonderful work."

"Thank you, but—"

"No. I shall not let you dissuade me. It's the least I can do to thank you for your hospitality."

Three days later, Elizabeth rode out with her retinue. Peace was restored to the house and Ursula felt exhaustion setting in. She would rather spend all day in bed than go about her daily chores.

One of her greatest pleasures was tending the rose garden. For now the plants were young, but they would be beautiful when they bloomed in summer. Together with a gardener, she'd also designed a beautiful knot garden and enjoyed seeing the progress as the sprigs of yew grew. Eventually they would be large enough to trim into neat hedges.

Deciding to be practical, Ursula had selected a variety of herbs to plant among the carefully selected flowers. Bay leaves and rosemary were destined for her kitchens, and some of the flowers could be collected and distilled into sweet-smelling perfumes. Her favourites were the fragrant white lilies currently in bloom.

It was a far cry from the beautiful gardens at Penshurst Place, or even Thornbury, but it brought her joy to sit out here and watch the bumblebees buzzing from flower to flower, while birdsong filled the air.

Harry's distant call interrupted her reverie and she turned to go back into the castle.

Ursula picked at the eel on her plate. "Are you certain it hasn't gone off?" she asked her husband.

He stole another morsel from her plate. "I am," he said, smiling. "If you don't like it, I will happily eat it for you."

Ursula picked at it for a moment more before sliding the plate towards him. Henry had ridden home from Grey's Inn to spend some time with the family and see to his business affairs. A long list of disputes between tenants was waiting. Although Ursula dealt with most of them herself, some required his personal attention.

"I attended the great ceremony in which the King invested Henry Fitzroy with his titles. He's now Duke of Richmond and Somerset."

"I heard it was being planned, but I wasn't sure the King would go through with it. I suppose his new household and lands will be paid for with money from your father's treasury."

Henry grimaced but agreed with her. "As long as the King is content with what he has taken and doesn't seek to claw back any of his generous gifts." He glanced around the hall, looking pleasantly surprised by the changes he had come home to. Bit by bit, Staffordshire Castle was becoming a more comfortable place to live. A home they weren't ashamed of.

"Your brother tells me the Queen has taken it badly and made a fuss," he said.

She sniffed. "I would too, if my legitimate child with my husband was overlooked."

Henry reached over to give her hand a squeeze. "It's mere politics. Without a legitimate son, the smart move would be to favour a bastard."

"I will pray for the security of the realm," Ursula said primly.

The following morning, unable to sleep, she rose at dawn and went out into the herb garden, checking on the progress of her plants. Back indoors, she nibbled on bread fresh from the oven, then went to check on Harry. On the way, she spied Henry speaking to her chambermaid.

"Henry?"

The chambermaid ran off, leaving Henry and Ursula alone in the corridor. Her eyes narrowed. "What were you doing?"

"I never thought you were a suspicious wife," he said, tapping her nose with a finger.

Ursula glared up at him. "I am serious, Henry."

"Have I ever been so disrespectful to you as to seduce your maids?"

"Perhaps you've learned from the King," she huffed indignantly.

"Hush, wife. I was merely inquiring about your well-being."

"Whatever for?"

He gave her an indulgent look, the sort he usually reserved for Harry. "It has come to my attention that you've been unwell. At the very least, you have lost your appetite."

Ursula shrugged. "I've been busy, but I am fine."

"Your chambermaid mentioned you've missed your courses."

"Again, not unusual." She frowned. "I will not be dictated to by a man who has never had them. They can become irregular when a woman is under stress, or tired. And at the moment you are making me both."

"Or it could be that you are pregnant and should take better care of yourself." He cocked his head to the side, grinning at her. "You know, usually it is the wife that gives the husband this news, not the other way around."

She flushed. "Henry, I don't think—" She stopped, counting the weeks. A spark of hope ignited inside as it dawned on her he could be right. Her hand flew to her flat belly. Could her prayers have been answered?

"It could just be a delay. It happened after your father's death. I don't want to raise our hopes over nothing."

"Very well," he said, placing a tender kiss on her cheek. "You must write to me the moment you are certain." He left her standing dumbfounded in the corridor, whistling a merry tune as he went.

Not long after Henry's departure, the castle received another visitor. Ursula's mother, the Countess of Salisbury, arrived with an escort wearing the bright blue and yellow livery of the Princess Mary.

"I was on my way to Ludlow to prepare for the Princess's arrival, when I thought I might take a detour to see you," she said, as she was helped down from her horse.

"You honour me, Lady Mother," Ursula said, curtseying low. When she rose up, her mother put a hand to her cheek, studying her.

"You are blossoming here," she said earnestly.

Ursula chuckled. "Indeed, in more ways than one," she said, and placed a hand on her belly. It had been two months since she'd last seen her husband and her courses had not come. Ursula had still not written to him, deciding to wait until she felt the child quicken within her.

"Congratulations," her mother said, arching an eyebrow. "When are you due?"

"Sometime in February or March. To be honest, I hadn't been keeping careful track of my days. I considered myself barren."

Her mother tutted disapprovingly. "Nonsense. You are a Plantagenet, as fertile as the common weed."

Ursula scoffed. "Common indeed. We have been humbled as you can see, but we are making the most of what we have left. How come the King has decided to send Princess Mary to Ludlow? Is he going to name her Princess of Wales?"

Her mother shook her head, her expression grim. "No, but it is a step in that direction. Let's take a turn about your lovely estate. I would like to see all the improvements you've been making."

Leaving her mother's escort to see to the horses, they found a secluded bench in the garden, away from listening ears.

"Your brother's wife is with child again. I pray on my hands and knees every day that she gives him a son. I wish to know I leave behind a stable succession to my lands."

"Mother, you are as strong as you ever were," Ursula said. It was true that her mother had aged. She was over fifty, with grey hair and wrinkled hands, but there was still a vitality to her that made her seem half her age.

"You need not flatter me. But in any case, I am glad you shall have another child of your own. Children are a blessing, though they can give you plenty of trouble."

"Has Geoffrey been gambling again?" Ursula guessed.

Lady Margaret nodded, chuckling to herself. "Your brother has the tastes of a king. He gambles and drinks the day away when he ought to be making himself useful. But he is a young nobleman without direction."

"You indulge him," Ursula said, thinking that by his age she already had a son.

"At this point, I think I tolerate him. He's over twenty. It's high time he did something with himself. Once the Princess is settled I will set about finding him a wife."

"And that will solve your problems?"

Her mother gave her a rare smile. "At the very least I'll have another pair of eyes to keep a watch on him."

"How is the Queen?" Ursula ventured to ask.

"Well enough. Already missing her daughter. I don't believe she imagined the King would send Mary away. She had hoped he would name her officially as his heir, but he has chosen this middle ground. However, it will be good for the Princess to learn statecraft."

"It will be a lot for one so young."

"She will manage, and she will have my caring guidance. The Queen has instructed me on how she wishes her daughter's household to be run and I will diligently obey every command."

"You are happy to be running her household, are you not?"

Her mother looked at her incredulously. "I was honoured when the Queen asked me to return to my post as the Princess's governess. I had no hesitation in agreeing." A courtier's answer.

Ursula suspected her mother would've preferred to

remain at Warblington, enjoying her twilight years in quiet retirement. But at the same time, her ambition was such that she could not let such an opportunity pass her by.

Before her mother left, Ursula packed away the very best of the mulberry crop they had picked and a few jars of marmalade she had personally made, as gifts for the Princess.

Ursula was soaking in a warm bath, inhaling the scent of lavender she'd add to the water.

She was exhausted. Against her better judgment she'd ridden out to check on the crops and speak to the farmers about their concerns.

The river was threatening to overflow its banks. Drainage ditches would have to be dug to protect the field; beyond that, only prayer could save them from the disaster of a flood.

Her maid brought forth a precious bar of Castile soap. Ursula inhaled the heady sandalwood scent. She used this only on special occasions, trying to make it last as long as possible. Imported from Spain, it had been a gift from her husband after he'd returned from London. Perhaps they should've saved the money, but these small luxuries were like a balm, smoothing over the hardships of everyday life.

After she had finished scrubbing away the dust and dirt that had settled on her, she climbed out of the tub and wrapped herself in towels.

Her hands drifted to her belly, which was starting to curve, the telltale sign that a child was growing within. She had not felt it move yet, which worried her. She prayed this pregnancy wouldn't end in a miscarriage.

"I hope I can tell your father about you soon," she whispered to her belly.

Harry ran ahead of her on the path, jumping from stone to stone.

"Look at me, Mama," he said, and then repeated himself in French.

Ursula smiled indulgently and watched as he ran back towards her. He pulled on her hands, urging her to hurry.

"Why are you so slow?" He gave a little pout.

Ursula knew she should scold him, but couldn't find it in her heart to do so. It was September, and the apples growing in the tiny orchard outside the castle gates were nearly ready to harvest.

"I have been unwell, Harry," she said, hoping it would jog his memory.

"Nurse says you are to have a baby," he said curiously, looking at her as though she might produce one from thin air.

"She shouldn't have said such things to you, but in all likelihood she is correct."

Harry grew pensive as he considered this. "I hope it's a brother and I hope he comes soon because I would like someone to play with. Someone fast, like me."

Ursula couldn't help but smile. "I shall do my best. But it is in God's hands. Perhaps you can help me write to your father later today. You can show him how you've improved with your letters."

"I can write out my name, and the Lord's Prayer." He puffed out his chest proudly.

Ursula kissed the top of his head. He was already up to her hip. At this rate he would be even taller than his father. Where had the time gone? She still remembered how he fit comfortably in the crook of her arms.

When they reached the fish pond, Harry asked to skip stones across the water and made a game of using a bullrush to fish. With his governess close at hand, Ursula retreated to sit on a stone bench nestled between the rose bushes.

Her attention shifted from her son to the beautiful roses around her. They were still blooming, and every time the lazy breeze blew past, Ursula would smell their delicate perfume.

She reached over to touch one of the blood red petals. It was like touching velvet. Contentment filled her as she considered how she might embroider them onto a cushion or have them painted on canvas.

Curious to see how the other varieties were faring, she stood. It was then she felt a fluttering in her stomach. She froze, and her hand flew to her belly. There it was again — that familiar sensation that told her life was growing within her. A radiant smile spread across her features and she felt like laughing.

Oh how she wished Henry was here to share in the moment.

That afternoon, once the household had settled, she pulled out a sheet of parchment and wrote to her husband.

The following morning she sent the letter by messenger to him in London.

She expected a quick reply, but none came.

Just over a week later, however, while she was working in the solar sewing a linen shirt for Harry, she heard footsteps. When she looked up she was surprised to see Henry standing in the doorway, still wearing a travelling cloak and cap.

He grinned at her expression and came forward to take her into his arms.

"What are you doing here? I thought you couldn't get away again until December."

"I had to see you for myself. You seem eager to conceal everything from me."

She gave him a light shove, but didn't pull away from his warm embrace. "I am well, as you can see."

"I wanted to be certain." He kissed her lips, then released her and urged her to sit down.

"You act as though I'm an invalid." She rolled her eyes.

"It was Harry who told me you were tired. He's out in the courtyard kicking a leather ball around."

Ursula's brow furrowed. "He should be studying."

Henry was far more indulgent. "Let him enjoy the nice weather. There will be plenty of time for him to sit with his books when winter descends upon us."

"And who will pay for the candles he needs?"

"I never thought you'd become so miserly. You made quite the argument for refurnishing your apartment at Penshurst for the second time."

"I was foolish, and didn't realise that our good fortune couldn't last forever."

They ate dinner together in private, with Harry doing his best to show he was mature and could sit still for longer than five minutes. But as expected, he shifted in his seat and made a mess with his food.

Ursula would've sent him to finish his meal in his own rooms, but it was a special occasion and they ought to be together. She watched as her husband gently tried to correct him.

When he looked up again, he gave a shake of his head and joked, "Perhaps the next one won't be such a wild animal."

After the dishes were cleared away, they sat together in the solar. Henry showed Harry how to roast chestnuts, and entertained him with tales of King Arthur.

"More," Harry said, rubbing his eyes with his hands.

"The volume is here in the library. If you apply yourself you can read it whenever you please."

Harry thought this was a very good idea and leapt to his feet. "Where's my tutor, Lady Mother?"

Ursula laughed. "I think he's asleep in his bed, which is exactly where you should be. Now go to your room and say your prayers. Tomorrow your father is leaving us bright and early and we want to be awake to bid him farewell."

Harry's eyes watered, but at a warning look from her he blinked away his disappointment.

Henry's eyes followed his little son as he left. "We must be doing something right if he wishes to be with us."

"We are indulgent parents who dote on him. But he's a

good boy. Rambunctious and full of energy, but we cannot blame him for that."

"Time is passing us by far too swiftly. I remember when he took his first tentative steps around the garden. Now he asks me for a pony to ride," Henry said, running a hand through his hair.

"You talk as though you are an old man approaching retirement."

They left the servants to put out the fire and retired for the evening. In a gauzy nightgown and a robe, she sat with her feet up by the fire. Henry came in to join her. His expression was pensive as he stared into the flames.

She was about to ask him what was on his mind when she felt another flutter in her belly and gave a start.

His attention snapped to her in a moment. "Is it the child?" he asked, coming close. "Should I summon the doctor?"

"No. Our child is moving. It merely surprised me."

"You can feel it already?" he asked, considering her.

She pulled aside her robe and pressed his hand into the curve of her belly. He looked at her uncertainly.

"Wait and you shall — ah, there it is. Did you feel that?"

"A ripple."

"Yes, that's it," Ursula said, grinning up at him. "Soon it will grow more obvious and then like with Henry, you will feel our child kick."

He knelt in front of her and placed a kiss on her belly. "Don't torment your mother."

She chuckled, ruffling his hair. "I don't mind. It reassures me that all is well. What had you looking so serious a moment ago?"

"The King has signed a peace treaty with the Emperor. There might be war."

"Will you have to go to France again?" A wave of worry hit her.

"If I am summoned I will go, but I won't volunteer myself. I have become as studious as a monk. So much for the warrior you married."

She grinned. "I prefer you here at my side."

The following day, she dressed Harry in his best clothes and took extra care with her toilette. This pregnancy had indeed left her feeling tired all the time, and she feared the dark circles under her eyes made her look frightful.

They stood in the courtyard watching him go. He doffed his cap and waved it as he rode away.

CHAPTER 15

1525

On 29 September, quarter day, it was left to Ursula as the Lady of the Household to collect the rents. The tenants rarely had the excuse or opportunity to gather together at the castle, so it was a chance to celebrate their hard work this year. As the landlord, Ursula provided casks of ale and food for all. The fare was not as grand as it had been at other times, but there was plenty of bread and hard cheese for everyone. A large pot of stew bubbled away in the kitchen, ready to be served.

Ursula had directed the servants to hang ribbons from the trees and hired entertainment for the day. There would be jugglers and minstrels, as well as an amateur troupe of actors to perform a short comedy. Lastly, she'd given permission for travelling merchants and farmers to set up stalls outside the castle gates. Everything from bolts of wool and silk ribbons to meat pies was for sale.

As her mother liked to point out, the holiday with free ale and food helped to ease the pain of paying their rents.

With her husband absent it was also up to Ursula to sit

at the great table with the large ledger book, to record what was collected. Tenant farmers could pay their rents with livestock or other produce from their farms. It was important to keep track of everything and to know the value as well. Behind her, the steward stood ready to give advice if she needed it.

Once she was done, Ursula planned on taking Harry out among the people to enjoy the festivities. Since his father had left there hadn't been many opportunities for him to enjoy himself.

One by one the tenants approached. She made little marks on the ledger beside their names, and motioned for the poorer tenants to go to the kitchens, where she had directed her staff to hand out little gifts, perhaps a bolt of homespun wool or a sack of grain.

She enjoyed being generous but knew charity had to have its limits if she was to keep her own household well fed this winter. There was also the new child to think of. They would need a crib, linen for swaddling bands, more staff. The numbers made her head spin and she pushed them aside to refocus on the task in front of her.

At last they were done. The coins had been locked in a chest and it was left to the steward to safely store it away. Sacks of goods and livestock were slowly being removed by servants who were already half-drunk on strong ale. When one fell over a fattened pig, she reprimanded him with a sharp look.

"Mother, is it time to go yet?" Her son had been sitting on a stool beside her so all their tenants could see their future landlord. She was proud of how patient he had been.

"Certainly, darling." She struggled to get to her feet.

She was four or five months along at most, but the baby was sitting in an odd position that set shooting pain up her back.

"Mother?"

Ursula looked down to see his concerned little face peering up at her.

"Not to worry. My legs just fell asleep from all that sitting."

"It's because of your big belly. You should not eat anymore pies," was his sage advice.

She smiled. "I should tell your father we have no need for a physician when you are near at hand. But no, this belly isn't because of pies. Your baby brother or sister is growing inside me. Remember?"

A flash of memory struck him and he nodded slowly. "Hopefully, he will come out soon." And, selfish as any child that age, he added, "He has been keeping me waiting a long time and he's making you slow too."

With a secret smile she led him away. They were accompanied by a guard, a maid who carried a purse of coins for their purchases, and Harry's nursemaid in case he took off running.

There was so much to see and do, and Harry ran to and fro from one stall to the next, pointing out little trinkets he wished to buy. Ursula laughed, but she didn't indulge him.

From one of her tenant farmers she bought two honey cakes, and they ate the sticky treats while watching a juggler perform in the temporary pavilion. Harry's features were alight with excitement, and when the juggler dropped his balls and did a somersault, he laughed with such glee it brought tears to his eyes. Seeing how happy he was made

Ursula's heart swell with joy. She wrapped a hand around him and pulled him close.

"I love you," she whispered, but her words were drowned out by the roar of the crowd.

Henry returned for the Christmas season bearing gifts.

"A bolt of beautiful green taffeta for your mother," he said to Harry, "and for you..." He paused, looking at his son's anxious face. "What do I have for you?" He made a great show of pretending he'd forgotten.

Harry's lower lip trembled, but he held back his tears and didn't throw a tantrum as he might have done a few months ago.

"Come with me," Henry said, and led him outside to the courtyard where a fat little pony was waiting.

"For me?" Harry clapped his hands in delight.

"Yes," Henry said, resting a hand on his tiny shoulders. "You will have to take lessons, and do not think of sneaking off to the stables alone to see him. He might be small but his hooves could still hurt you."

Ursula watched as Henry helping Harry into the saddle. Her mind was hazy these days and it was making her sluggish.

"I have a pony of my very own, Lady Mother," Harry said, shouting with glee. His father showed him how to hold the reins, then took the lead and urged the pony forward. They circled the courtyard once and then a second time at Harry's urging.

The pony was old but still strong and steady, perfect for a first-time rider.

Henry pulled his son off its back and Ursula held out her arms to him.

He ran towards her. "Did you see how brave I was? I sat still in the saddle just like Father told me to."

"I am very proud of you," Ursula said, kissing his cheek. "You must be sure to thank your father."

"He says once I learn to ride, I can start training to joust." Harry's eyes were bright orbs. "I will be a knight one day, just wait and see."

Ursula's heart clenched at his words. She knew what that meant, even if he didn't. It wasn't like the chivalric tales. One mistake could cost you your life. She tried not to imagine the day when her son would ride off to war. It filled her with fear.

Henry approached and sensing her mood, put a comforting hand on her shoulder. "Don't worry, there are years before he is old enough for such things. But it will be his duty to fight for his country should the need arise."

Harry overheard this and pouted. "It won't be long. In two years I'll be grown."

His father glared at him. "In two years, you will be lucky if you can gallop around the yard on your own."

Harry stomped his foot and stormed off.

"That's the thanks I get?" Henry said, but his irritation was tempered by amusement.

Before it grew dark outside, they retreated to Henry's office where they sat looking over their ledgers and documents, trying to reconcile their household accounts. As always the numbers were tight.

"This can't be right," Ursula said.

Henry rubbed the back of his neck as he sat back looking at the final figure. "No, everything's in order. But feel free to double check the numbers."

"We won't be able to be so generous with our tenants come next quarter day," Ursula said, biting a finger as she tried to calculate the money they would receive the next quarter day.

"We'll manage. We always have."

Henry was trying reassure her, but Ursula shook her head. "You didn't need that hunter. Perhaps we can sell him. And Harry's pony. It was a wonderful gift, but it will cost a fortune to keep him fed through the winter when he won't be able to graze."

"Ursula." He reached for her but she swatted his hand away.

"This is serious," she said, tapping her finger on the account book. "How will we ever save for our son's future?"

Henry's good-natured disposition melted away and his smile twisted into a scowl. "We live like beggars already. I will not become some old miser hoarding his coins. Harry is reaching an age when he will have to begin his training with a marshal. I won't have him brought up like the son of a merchant."

Ursula's own anger flared. "He shouldn't be encouraged to joust. It's dangerous and expensive. It's bad enough that he needs to learn how to wield a sword."

"He would be a laughingstock."

"Among who?" Ursula made a show of looking around the empty room. "He will grow up to be a respectable country gentleman. That is not such a terrible future."

"He should have more. I am working hard to try to recover what we have lost. I dream of greater things for our son than living a quiet life in the middle of nowhere."

"Are you truly so unhappy here, Henry?" she asked, eyes downcast. "We have our health, we have food on the table and each other. Do you still cling to dreams of grandeur? I thought we'd moved past that. We will never be welcomed as courtiers. The King will not restore you." Her bitter laugh at his stunned expression echoed around the room. "Henry, he has given out all the valuable castles and lands to his friends. The rest he has kept for himself and his bastard son. We are left with the scraps. He won't take from his friends to give to us." She shook her head.

Henry got to his feet, his eyes filled with anger. "I bid you good evening, madam." He stormed out of his office and Ursula didn't try to stop him. She regretted being cruel, but it grated on her nerves that he was so blasé about everything. Henry needed to face reality or they would never move forward.

They didn't speak to each other for the rest of the week, a feat that was difficult to accomplish given the weather trapped them indoors.

It was only when Harry fell ill with a fever that they came together.

"He's burning up," Ursula said, her eyes filling with tears as she regarded her son where he tossed and turned in his bed.

Henry wrapped an arm around her. "The doctor is on his way. We must be strong for him."

She buried her face in his shoulder and wept. "I'm sorry."

"This wasn't your doing." He patted her back.

"I am sorry we fought. This is God's punishment on us."

"Ursula." He put his hand under her chin and lifted her head up to look at him. "Children get sick all the time. You are a wonderful mother to our son and a good wife to me. We quarrelled. It was a mistake and I'm sorry too."

Together they tended their precious son. Ursula was nearing her time, and often could do no more than sit by Harry's side, praying over his little body as he slept.

A week after Harry fell sick, Ursula was aware of her mind wandering. Fatigue had entered her bones, and no matter how many layers she wore, she shivered.

Still she refused to leave Harry's side.

The doctor urged Henry to be more insistent with her, and he knelt at her feet. "Ursula, my love, you are ill."

"Harry needs me."

"And our other child needs you too." He placed a hand on her protruding belly as though to remind her. "You must go and rest."

After more cajoling she finally agreed.

Ursula never felt so bad in her life. Like Harry, she began drifting in and out of fever.

This was no way to spend the Christmas season.

One morning she awoke to find her mind finally clear of

the haze that had held her in its grip. She was weak but her hand immediately went to her belly. She felt her child push against her stomach, and smiled.

Still exhausted she turned her head, and was surprised to find Elizabeth sleeping at her bedside.

"Elizabeth," she said, her voice hoarse. Had she been sleeping for long?

Her sister-in-law was at her side in an instant. "Ursula, you are awake!" There were tears in her eyes.

"What has happened? Where is Harry?"

"He's fine. Recovering, thank God. You fell into a deep sleep and the doctors worried this illness would—" She couldn't finish the thought. Elizabeth held her hand and brought it to her lips. "I am so glad you are awake. Henry has been beside himself. We thought for sure you'd lose the baby."

"I felt her moving."

"Her?" Elizabeth arched her brow.

Ursula shrugged. "Just a feeling."

"You had some spotting. But that stopped once the fever abated. Henry wrote to me the moment you took to your bed. I came as soon as I could. Is there anything you need?"

"Water," Ursula said, her head pounding with every word she spoke.

Elizabeth stuck her head out the door and shouted something.

Moments later, Henry and a troop of servants entered. He helped prop her up and held the glass to her lips when she was too weak to do so herself.

"I am so glad you've come back to us," Henry said, kissing her brow. "The doctor has recommended a diet of porridge and as much meat as you can manage, to build up your strength."

She looked beyond him to see the servants carrying trays of food. "I cannot possibly eat all that."

"I didn't know what you might prefer, so I had them make one of everything."

"You fool," she said, but she chuckled. "Thank you."

"Thank Elizabeth, I would've been lost without her," he said, though it must have pained him to admit it.

"I would like to see Harry if I can," Ursula said, a sense of urgency in her voice.

Not long after, her son came running to her bedside. He was thinner than before he took ill, but his exuberant energy was restored.

"You look well," she said, placing a hand on his cheek. "You gave us quite a scare."

Harry looked like he was about to cry and she hurried to reassure him. "I am not mad at you. I love you." He hugged her and began sobbing into her neck. "Hush now, child. All is well. We must give thanks for our good fortune."

"Harry, why don't you help your mother eat some food?" Elizabeth suggested, putting a hand on his back. "She and the baby must be very hungry."

And so it was that Ursula was served like a queen. A duchess wiped her chin, while a nobleman's son spoon-fed her hot porridge. The nobleman held her up for support.

Day by day Ursula grew stronger, and by the end of the week could move about on her own. Now she spent most of her days sitting in the parlour doing her needlework for as long as the light of day allowed.

Elizabeth had been her constant companion, but Ursula

grew worried she was becoming an inconvenience. "I am nearly back to my old self again. Soon I will have to go into confinement and face the travails of childbirth. You ought to go home."

Elizabeth looked up from her book.

"I am quite determined to be with you until you are safely delivered of your child." The stubborn set of her mouth told Ursula she wouldn't be sent away.

"If you are certain."

"I am a duchess. You'd dare question me?" She put her hand to her chest in mock outrage.

"Oh no," Ursula said with a laugh. "Never."

"Good." Elizabeth grinned and snapped open her book again.

"She's perfect," Henry said, kissing his daughter's forehead.

"All ten fingers and toes accounted for," Elizabeth said, in a business-like manner.

"I hope she'll have your eyes, Henry. By the looks of it, it's entirely possible." Ursula held her hands out for her daughter. She looked down, marvelling at the little miracle in her arms.

"All babies have blue eyes," Elizabeth said curtly. Then, realising the beaming parents wouldn't appreciate her comments, she shut her mouth and returned to arranging the linens in the crib. "But she is especially blessed."

Indeed, a saint must have been watching over her. She had been born on a saint's day, and survived her mother's fever. And she had quickened while her mother was in the garden. There had been no disagreement about what her name should be.

"You'll have to excuse your aunt," Ursula said to the baby in her arms. "She doesn't understand the joy you bring me."

Her husband leaned over to add, "Us."

Their daughter gave a great big yawn.

"She is tired. Bless her, she's had a long day eating and sleeping," Ursula said, getting to her feet. Taking the greatest care she placed her in the intricately carved cradle her mother had lent them.

Elizabeth took a seat, using her foot to rock the infant as though it was the most natural thing in the world for her to be doing. Henry came over and wrapped an arm around Ursula as they stared down at their daughter, who fought to keep her eyes open and failed.

All three hovered, leaning in to observe the baby's peaceful face and the rise and fall of her chest. Ursula took over rocking and sent the other two from the room.

She would never get tired of watching her daughter sleep. She moved in her crib, and Ursula began humming a lullaby. At last she fell into a deep slumber.

Ursula whispered, "Sweet dreams, Dorothy."

AUTHOR'S NOTE

Ursula and Henry would go on to have at least fourteen children. Their fortune was never fully restored, but over the years they managed to reclaim more of their lost lands. During the rule of Edward VI, Henry was created 1st Baron Stafford.

They always had money troubles, regardless of their income. I have suggested in this book that this was due to a desire for extravagance, as well as finding it difficult to accept a diminished station in life.

Elizabeth Stafford, Duchess of Norfolk, infamous for her tumultuous marriage to the Duke of Norfolk, remained close friends with Ursula throughout their lives. She took Dorothy and another of Ursula's daughters into her household, ostensibly to educate them and provide them with a better future. Not only would this give them opportunities, it would also to help reduce the cost of Ursula's household. Elizabeth's own children were estranged from her. Her daughter Mary is the main character in my novel *The Lady's Defiance*.

At the time, the arrest and execution of the Duke of Buckingham was shocking, especially the attainder that impoverished his heir. There was no concrete proof he had committed treason or was planning to. Merely boasting or discussing his closeness to the throne was not at a crime (at the time). However, no one would disobey the king.

Ursula's mother was the tragic Countess of Salisbury, who King Henry VIII arrested and executed to the horror of his subjects, as she was in her sixties by this time.

Ursula would outlive all her siblings and be the only one of them to see the last Tudor monarch, Queen Elizabeth I, come to her throne.

Both Ursula and her husband Henry lived into their sixties, dying within a few years of each other.

Of all Ursula's children, Dorothy is perhaps the most famous. Once Queen Elizabeth I took the throne she was a lady of the bedchamber and eventually rose to the influential position of Mistress of the Robes. The Feast of Saint Dorothy was traditionally in February. She was known as the patroness saint of gardeners and was often depicted holding roses. I decided to incorporate that into this story as a way to account for the uncommon name choice.

You can read her story in my standalone novel: *The Lady of Fortune* (part of my other series, Ladies of the Golden Age, and written in first person).

Printed in Great Britain
by Amazon

38351922R00128